License To Convict

A Novel

Carroll Multz

License to Convict

Revised Edition

Published by
ShahrazaD Publishing
859 Quail Run Dr.
Grand Junction, CO 81505

ISBN: 978-164764000-2
ISBN: 978-1-62024-033-5

1 Fiction/Legal 2 Fiction/Suspense

Contact the author at:
carrollmultz@charter.net

Also By Carroll Multz

Adult Novels

Justice Denied · Deadly Deception
The Devil's Scribe · The Chameleon
Shades of Innocence · The Winning Ticket

With Judith Blevins

Rogue Justice · The Plagiarist · A Desperate Plea
Spiderweb · The Mejico Connection · Lust for Revenge
Eyewitness · Kamanda · Bloodline · Pickpocket
Ghost Writer

Childhood Legends Series®
A series of novels for middle-grade readers
With Judith Blevins

Operation Cat Tale · One Frightful Day · Blue
The Ghost of Bradbury Mansion · White Out
A Flash of Red · Back in Time · Treasure Seekers
Summer Vacation – Part 1: Castaways - Part 2: Blast Off

Dedication

*This book is dedicated
to my father, Edwin E. Multz,
a prosecutor who never
betrayed the public's trust,
and to prosecutors
like him everywhere.*

*Freedom must rest
on the integrity of
just prosecution.*

— Campaign Slogan of Author —

TABLE OF CONTENTS

LICENSE TO CONVICT — CARROLL MULTZ

A Note From The Author

Justice has been described by some legal scholars as an ideological concept. Having been a part of the criminal justice system as a city attorney, district attorney, assistant attorney general, defense attorney, and judge, I'm here to tell you that justice is more than fanciful speculation.

Although the novel you are about to read is reflective of a writer's imagination, it was inspired by cases in which I was involved or with which I was familiar. That is as far as the similarities will be found. The primary setting of License to Convict is a nonexistent part of Colorado with totally fictitious characters involved in wholly contrived events. The outcomes, it is hoped, are due to more than wishful thinking, rhetorical hyperbole, or divine providence.

The temptations with power are real. This novel is truly dedicated to the incorruptible — those who, despite the inevitable enticements, choose to operate at the highest possible level. The main character I've created herein is not an enigma but representative of the prosecutors with whom I have worked and come to respect and admire. May prosecutors always be of the caliber their constituents desire and deserve.

The lessons I've learned and am still learning started with an honorable, uncompromising father who was the quintessential prosecuting attorney, continued with those who accompanied me on my fifty-year criminal law journey, and are nearing an end with those who are traveling with me now. Those lessons are what define me and are what are reflected herein. May justice be as near and dear to you as these pages you read and the air you breathe. Embrace it with all your might.

I'm eternally grateful to the publishers of this edition and its predecessor. Thanks also to my daughter, Lisa Knudsen, Judy Blevins, Amber Burnell, Sheri Davis and Margie Vollmer Rabdau, for their input and professional skills in preparation of the manuscript. Their encouragement and prodding and that of my daughter, Natalie Lowery, were the catalytic agents responsible for completion of this undertaking.

But for the inspiration of my fellow prosecutors throughout the years, I would not have had the incentive to write such a novel. To them and to all those who have accompanied me on my journey in criminal law, I am most grateful.

It is only fitting that I single out and pay tribute to the man who taught me the noble art of criminal prosecution—the man in whose honor the Hall of Justice in Colorado Springs, Colorado, was named. To Robert L. Russel, I convey my profound admiration and appreciation not just for the effect he had on my professional career but my personal life as well. Serving as Bob's Chief Trial Deputy from 1968 to 1972 was a life-altering experience. I can never thank him enough.

Finally, to the designer of the cover and interior of the revised edition, Frank Addington, my profound thanks.

Additional Remarks: Although the first edition of *License to Convict* was heralded for its technical approach, it has been rewritten to appeal to a wider base. The same is true of its predecessors, *Justice Denied* and *Deadly Deception*. No longer pedagogical in nature, the three are still designed to inform, inspire, and entertain—in that order. For those who are intrigued by courtroom drama, I have left the court scenes virtually untouched. Sit back and enjoy!

CHAPTER 1

Righteous Indignation

Have you ever felt like you had just been stabbed in the heart and that the world around you had just collapsed? That's the way Morris Bradley Dexter felt as the verdict was being read. As a prosecuting attorney, the two words you never want to hear are *not guilty*. Morrey, as he was called, was stunned by the verdict, and even when it was repeated by his investigator, thought his ears were playing deceptively cruel tricks.

Once reality set in, Morrey, flushed and frustrated, turned to Toby Kincaid, his lifelong friend and first appointee upon being elected DA, and stammered, "My God, Toby, what kind of verdict is that? The imbecile, by sending his thirteen-year-old diabetic daughter off to a health ranch, in essence sentenced her to death. Allowing the substitution of health formulas for insulin, in my book, is criminally negligent homicide and plain and simple, unadulterated child abuse."

Toby was stunned. He'd never seen Morrey like this. Under pressure, Morrey was ordinarily unflappable. It was almost as if he snapped.

Concerned and frightened as to what Morrey might do, Toby put a calming hand on Morrey's forearm and whispered, "You can't be a virgin your whole career as a prosecutor. You can't expect to win them all! This was a tough one, and the jury bought the defense argument that the father's desperation resulted in an error in judgment."

"The verdict is an abominable and detestable message to send to the community," Morrey, refusing to be consoled, managed to whisper back. "You can gamble on your child's life, and if it results in her death, it's okay as long as you had good intentions. I don't buy it and can't accept the concept that bad choices shouldn't result in consequences, particularly when they result in someone else's death. And don't tell me you don't feel the same way!"

Toby sat in silence and listened to Morrey vent his anger and disbelief. He and Morrey had been friends for many years and Toby knew when to pursue an argument with Morrey and when to let go. He knew Morrey wouldn't back down. He respected Morrey for his deep-seated convictions and quest to rectify the world's wrongs. And even though Toby had a daughter the same age as the dead girl, he couldn't help but feel some empathy for the parents. *None of us know what medical alternatives we would pursue if we were desperate and in these parents' shoes*, Toby thought. He figured he might have done the same thing.

• • •

Courtroom protocol required the victorious courtroom gladiator to shake hands with his or her vanquished counterpart. It was usually Morrey who initiated the formalities, and he marveled at the graciousness of the loser as the latter accepted his outstretched hand. Today, however, would be different. Accepting defense counsel's condolences and obligatory platitudes was not palatable—not in this case, and maybe not in any case. Still displaying his disgust and indignation, Morrey quickly gathered up his files and hurried out of the courtroom before the victorious defense counsel could pack his briefcase and make the overture.

Toby was close behind. The prosecution team didn't have far to go. The courtrooms with attached judicial chambers were on the third floor. The district attorney's office was on the second floor, along with the county offices including the county commissioners' office and their hearing room. The first floor, which was partially underground, housed the county jail and the sheriff's department. In what was called the attic, accessible by a spiral staircase, was a rather extensive law library with two long end-to-end oak library tables surrounded by surprisingly comfortable old-fashioned oak armchairs.

The Paraiso County Courthouse or Hall of Justice, as it was sometimes called, was erected in the early 1880s and even by modern-day standards was stately and regal in appearance. The building's exterior was constructed of solid granite and was one of the few courthouses of that era that had been built with future expansion in mind.

One of the most distinguishing features was its portico with ornate pediment and Doric columns. This had been considered the only frivolous feature of this otherwise functional structure and is thought to have been the brainchild of the then eccentric chairperson of the board of county commissioners.

• • •

It was now after-hours when Toby unlocked the door to the DA's office. Painted in black lettering on the large window panel to the left of the door was:

Office of the District Attorney
Morris Bradley Dexter
District Attorney
Terrence R. Brockerton
Assistant District Attorney

Colorado was divided into judicial districts. There was an elected district attorney for each district. Some districts were multicounty. Morrey's district was comprised of only one county, Paraiso County. *Paraiso* was the Spanish word for paradise. Paraiso County sat in the northern part of the state, nestled in the bosom of the great Rocky Mountain range. Its northern border was the state of Wyoming.

The county seat of Paraiso County was Las Cruces. The county was known for its rich minerals, fertile farms, and immense cattle operations. It was established long before Colorado became a state and was known for its speedy and efficient administration of justice. Its mantra was: "Hang the crook and ask questions later." Las Cruces was named after the stone crosses that dotted the landscape and were the handiwork of a revered Spanish missionary by the name of Padre Vincente Rosario in the early 1800s. The crosses are thought to be monuments marking the graves of notorious outlaws who roamed the Wild West and who met their Waterloo at Las Cruces.

In fact, prior to Padre Rosario's arrival, Las Cruces was known as Tarugo, the Spanish word for wooden peg. Folklore has it that Tarugo inherited its name for its improvisation of the polygraph, or at least its forerunner. To determine if an accused who proclaimed his or her innocence was telling the truth, he or she was spread-eagle, and his or her hands and feet were bound with ropes tethered to wooden pegs or stakes. The Tarugo Polygraph was administered at noon on one day and concluded at noon on the following day. If the accused survived the elements and wild animals and was still alive at the end of the ordeal, he or she was determined to have passed the polygraph, and being thus vindicated, was set free.

For the early part of its existence, there was no courthouse in Paraiso County. There really was no need for one. The sheriff and his deputies were pretty much the judge, jury and executioners, and justice was dispensed onsite. That's assuming, of course, the criminal conduct was brought to the attention of the authorities in the first place. Even today, poachers and cattle rustlers are not processed through the criminal justice system. They just mysteriously disappear. The recidivism rate was low no doubt for that reason.

With that backdrop and the otherwise pervasive redneck mentality of the community, Morrey and Toby had more than just cause to question the nature of the verdict just rendered — Morrey more than Toby.

• • •

When the Paraiso County sheriff, Sergio Santana, let himself in the front office and found his way to Morrey's private office, he found Morrey slumped in the sagging seat of his decrepit red leather executive chair with his eyes closed and face pointed heavenward and Toby entwined in the paper heap on the old red leather sofa with a cold, wet washcloth draped over his head.

Neither looked up when they heard Sergio's booming voice, as both were familiar with the clatter of his boots announcing his arrival as he shuffled his way down the oak floor hallway. He sounded as if he had horseshoes nailed to his boots. Several times in the past, without receiving a reply, they asked who his blacksmith was. Also, they expected his usual caustic comments. Only this time, they knew they deserved them.

"Rumor has it you're every bit the quintessential poor loser," said Sergio glaring at the defeated prosecutor. To Toby, he said, "You remind me of my hypochondriacal great-aunt." Sergio continued to no one in particular, "I guess I could count on the district attorney's office screwing up a perfectly investigated and open-and-shut case."

"Is that any way to talk to your favorite son-in-law?" Morrey, now sitting forward on his chair and resting his chin on the palms of his hands, quipped.

"I'm going to walk down the street incognito

from now on, and if recognized, will deny you're married to my daughter," said Sergio, feigning indignation.

"We're so ashamed," Toby said sarcastically as he removed the washcloth from his head and looked into the dark, piercing eyes that dominated Sergio's dark, chiseled face.

That was the comic relief they all needed. However, the laughter was more contrived than heartfelt.

Morrey shook his head still disgusted at himself for having lost the case. "You deserve to have my head delivered on a platter," Morrey muttered to Sergio. "I guess we really let you, the sheriff 's department, and the community down on this one."

As gruff as he was, Sergio loved his son-in-law, and each had a great amount of respect for the other. Sergio was the father Morrey lost when he was only twelve. Morrey was the son Sergio never had.

Monique was the Santana's only child. She was a true Indian princess. She had been Morrey's love since first grade. Upon graduation from high school, they married. Morrey turned eighteen the following August and Monique that September. Morrey had been a three-year letterman in football, basketball, and track, as had Toby. Monique had been a cheerleader since her sophomore year as had her best friend, Camille, who was now married to Toby.

Although both couples attended the University of Colorado in Boulder, the couples, upon graduation, took different paths. The Kincaids returned to Las Cruces, where Toby became a deputy sheriff under Sergio and where he remained until Morrey was elected district attorney. The Dexters remained in Boulder, where Morrey attended law school, graduating three years later. Monique worked in a large law firm as a legal secretary, the same firm for whom Morrey law clerked, Forrester, Dunning, & Griffith. Upon Morrey passing the Colorado bar exam, the Dexters returned to Las Cruces, where Morrey practiced law on his own for four-and-a-half years before being elected district attorney.

Over the years, the Santanas, Dexters and Kincaids had shared the good times and the bad. Sergio had been a friend of Morrey's father and was a pallbearer at his funeral. The three had their share of family outings together at the Santana's summer home near Rocky Mountain National Park on the Hadow Mountain National Recreation Area side. It was still the favorite playground for the three and their families, including Morrey's mother and Toby's parents.

"You're not having second thoughts about not charging the girl's mother, are you, Morrey?" Sergio asked, as he positioned himself on the corner of Morrey's desk.

"Sergio, you saw her in court. She was frail and pitiful, a broken woman. You could tell who was in charge of that family. Her complicity, if any, in the so-called medical decision was not by commission but omission. I didn't have the heart to file charges on her."

"I don't think it would have had any bearing on the outcome if we had charged her," said Toby. "Her being charged would have only bolstered more sympathy for the now vindicated father."

"What bothered me most," Morrey admitted, "was watching that now daughterless couple embrace and celebrate the court victory as though they had just won the lottery."

"I think you misconstrued the mother's tears," Toby interjected. "I don't think they were tears of joy. I think they were tears of sorrow."

"I agree with Toby," said Sergio. "Watching the couple interact, I think she's sorry she's stuck with a poor excuse of a father and a husband. Besides, you succeeded in obtaining convictions on the pretend doctor and his pretend nurse at New Haven Health Ranch. Convictions on criminally negligent homicide and practicing medicine without a license place the blame on the most deserving." Looking thoughtful as he toyed with the letter opener on Morrey's desk, Sergio continued, "You exacted the perceived pound of flesh when each was sentenced to the maximum—three years in the Colorado State Penitentiary."

"I still can't erase from my memory," Morrey said, again shaking his head, "that precious teenage girl lying lifeless on that cold steel slab at the morgue."

"Nor can I," Toby added. "Remember, I have a daughter, my only child, who is the same age."

"Thirteen is way too young," Sergio said reflectively. "Morrey, your wife was thirteen once. Toby has a thirteen-year-old and you have nine and eleven-year-old daughters, my grand-daughters, who both will be thirteen before we know it. Despite your animosity toward the girl's father, even you will have to admit there was some validity in his meant well, just made a bad decision defense."

Morrey pushed his chair back and propped his feet up on his desk, as he asked, "Did you notice the disproportionate number of newcomers on the jury?" Before either Toby or Sergio could answer, he continued, "I mean, the longtime residents of our community were outnumbered. Quite frankly, the trend frightens me."

"I hear that! I'm told our population is now approaching sixty thousand. Only three years ago, it was less than thirty-five thousand," Sergio said as he moved to one of the chairs facing Morrey's desk. "I've felt the impact in the number of calls logged by my deputies, and we've all noticed the change in the public's temperament and attitude toward authority in general and law enforcement in particular."

"What bothers me," Toby interjected, "is the negative impact created by the change in demographics. The type of people who made our community the thriving community that it once was are dying out and the new breed, especially the transplants and carpetbaggers, have no regard for tradition and are transforming our once desirable community into a loathsome conclave. Pretty soon they will be changing the name of our county from Paraiso to Paraiso Perdido."

"Or something worse," Sergio added.

"Drastic times demand drastic measures," said Morrey as he sat forward and pounded his fist on the desk in symbolic resignation. They all knew what he meant, and all were thinking the same thing. Paraiso County would never be known as

Paradise Lost, not as far as they were concerned and not if they had anything to do about it. It was not in their temperament to stand idly by and let that happen.

CHAPTER 2

The Hit List

Christmas in Las Cruces was like no other anywhere in the hemisphere. It had biblical connotations and marked the traditional period of amnesty and reconciliation. There was peace in this part of the world and truly goodwill among all. It was a particularly sacred time for the Santana, Dexter, and Kincaid clans as they sat in church together celebrating the birth of the Messiah.

After the Christmas church service, family and friends gathered at the Santana casa. They were greeted by a twenty-foot Colorado Blue Spruce Christmas tree, resembling in breadth and beauty the one greeting guests this Christmas at the White House. It was not long before the great room looked like a war zone. Strewn around the room was torn wrapping paper, discarded ribbons of all descriptions, cardboard containers in various states of destruction and other items suggesting that Santa's gifts had been enthusiastically claimed and hastily whisked away.

There were approximately two-dozen partaking of the Christmas feast at the Santana casa. After dinner and the cleanup, the children retreated to the family room to get acquainted with their recently acquired gifts. As was their custom, the men retreated to Sergio's study.

Sipping brandy and standing in front of the fireplace in the study were Sergio, Morrey, Toby, Morrey's brother-in-law, Ramon, Morrey's secretary's husband, Kevin, and Toby's father, Milton. For years now, this had been the tradition. This was the third year in a row that "those nasty cigars," as the women called them, had been eliminated from their ritual. This year they also deviated from tradition in their discussion. Instead of debating the world problems, religion, politics, the economy, and other equally important topics, they focused on a new problem: newbies.

It started innocently enough. Sergio, with one foot planted on the hearth, asked Kevin how the hardware business had been going. Kevin was the manager of the family business started by his great-grandfather.

"Saunders Hardware has had more sales this year than any previous year," replied Kevin. "That's the good news. The bad news is profits are down because of shrinkage and bad checks."

"What do you attribute that to?" Milton innocently asked, as he swirled brandy around in his glass.

"Do you mean the shrinkage or the bad checks?"

"Both."

"We hired some new people we didn't know well, people who had just moved into town and who we hadn't bothered to check out. You know how trusting all of us have been in the past. Well, those days are apparently over. Several of the hires helped themselves to our inventory and stole us blind, but we can't prove it. The majority of the bad checks were written by people who had just moved into town and hadn't yet opened local bank accounts. We call it the *newbie syndrome*."

Squinting, Milton asked, "The what?"

"The newbie syndrome. You know, the influx of new people who seem to be taking over our town by storm."

"We were just talking about that the other day," Toby interrupted. "It's becoming a real problem."

"More than a real problem," said Morrey emphatically. "It's become an albatross around our necks and is literally strangling life out of this community."

"We found that out in the child killer case, didn't we?" Sergio said more as a statement than a question. "The jury was not the typical Paraiso jury, not in composition and not in result. It appears they gave a free pass to an otherwise guilty defendant."

Milton then asked Sergio if the steady rise in the crime rate in Las Cruces and the county was due to the newbies or some other extrinsic cause.

"Take a look at the blotter," Sergio responded. "How many names do you recognize? It's pretty obvious that most of our perpetrators are not indigenous to our community." Sergio, then gesturing in Morrey's direction, asked, "What element comprises the bulk of the DA's new filings?"

"I think the newbies are responsible for at least seventy-five to eighty percent of the crime rate," said Morrey.

"The crime rate here had been pretty low for a number of years," said Toby. "However, we've seen a recent surge with the migration of newcomers or newbies to our district. There seems to be a direct correlation between the number of incidents and contacts by law enforcement agencies and the changing demographics as people migrate to the newly discovered paradise."

"It's curious," Toby said reflectively, "how so many newbies ended up on the jury panel. No matter how many times the flip of the coin turns up heads, the chance that the next flip will turn up heads is still fifty percent."

"Ramon, you're a medical doctor," said Morrey. "We've diagnosed an ailment. What's the cure?"

"Your mantra," Ramon, apparently pleased at having finally been included in the discussion, replied, "has always been to *fight fire with fire*. The question is how to counteract the antisocial forces at work in our community. It seems as though the criminal element does not play by the rules. *What's good for the goose no longer appears to be good for the gander.* But, unfortunately, that's not the way it works. What's that other saying? *All's fair in love and war.* Maybe law enforcement should find a way to level the playing field."

"Morrey," Toby interjected, "wasn't it you who said drastic times demand drastic measures?"

Suddenly the ball was back in Morrey's court. He just sat there silently. His head was spinning. He had always played by the book. Looking at Toby's father, he was reminded of his own father's comment many years before when one of Morrey's classmates had taken advantage of him: *Nice guys finish last unless they resist and are otherwise assertive!* That certainly was the case lo those many years ago. *Things haven't changed much!* he thought and shook his head.

Although somewhat guarded, Sergio said he was resigned to the fact that the *good old days* and the *land of milk and honey* were things of the past and would soon be ancient history. He said the upstarts would soon be in the majority and that in a democracy, the will or voice of the majority would became the law. He concluded by saying that he was glad he was in the checkout lane and felt sorry for his grandchildren and great-grandchildren.

"It appears these days, we're all under public scrutiny and that everyone is looking at everything we do with a jaundiced eye," said Morrey. "How would you like to run for office every four years? Every time I, my assistant, or deputies walk into court, we evoke the ire of someone. Think about it. Just by filing charges, we have made enemies of the accused, his spouse, family, and friends. If we obtain a conviction, we're certainly in their crosshairs. If we *don't* obtain a conviction, the victim and his or her spouse, family, and friends become lifelong enemies. It's a no-win situation. Sooner or later, we're going to do something that offends someone and ultimately everyone—that is, if we do our job right. And by trying to please everyone, we please no one."

"If you stay in office long enough," said Toby, "chances are that you will not be reelected. The exception, of course, is someone like Sergio who has been elected or re-elected sheriff eight times."

"Multiply my four-year term by eight, and you'll have an idea of how long I will have been in office when my current term expires," said Sergio. "I've either done a good job or done a good job in not antagonizing anyone. I'm not a cat sitting on a hot tin roof like Morrey but I still have my share of detractors nonetheless."

"Speaking of detractors," Toby chimed in, "both Morrey and Sergio are up for reelection in less than a year and a half. Do you think the newbies have enough clout to get one of their own elected?"

Milton rubbed his brow in thoughtful reflection. "I've heard it said that the young attorney who moved in not far from my business, Shay Bisben, may be eyeing Morrey's position," said Milton. "I haven't, however, heard of anyone coveting Sergio's job."

"I don't think either of you have much to worry about," Ramon declared reassuringly.

"You never know, Ramon," Morrey replied. "We thought we had the last case in the bag, and the newbies literally clobbered us. That may happen again at election time."

"By the way, does anyone know anything about Shay Bisben or his background?" Ramon asked.

"Now that you ask, rumor has it that he was placed on a deferred judgment and sentence on some kind of drug charge before he moved here, but his record was wiped clean, and no one seems to want to talk about it," Toby replied. "Wonder who his connections are?"

"Can't your office or the sheriff 's department find out?" Ramon asked.

"Even if it's confirmed," Morrey responded, "we can't use it, and even if we could, I wouldn't stoop to that level. Besides, we're not even sure Bisben would run if I announced."

"You mean, *when* you announce," Milton corrected.

Morrey smiled at Milton's show of support. "With all that's transpiring in the county and the reluctance of the county commissioners to give my deputies and myself a reasonable raise, I'm not real anxious to succeed myself," Morrey responded shaking his head in disgust.

"With all that's going on in the county, we need you now more than ever," Sergio said emphatically. "I'm sure, with a little pressure, the county commissioners will come around. Otherwise, they'll be paying your replacement more to get less. If they haven't got the message by now, maybe we ought to think about replacing them." Then, turning to Milton, he added, "Milton, you'd make a great county commissioner."

"Thanks for your expression of faith. Even though I'd like to put Bisben and the county commissioners on the top of the *hit list*, I don't really want the job," Milton replied.

"Add Harvey Beckman, our antiquated county judge to the list," Toby suggested. "He has been rendering some weird decisions lately that are not exactly prosecution-friendly."

"I think we ought to start with the elusive criminals in our community whose cleverness and reliance on legal technicalities have shielded them from convictions, such as Morano Balken, the biggest drug dealer this side of the Rocky Mountains," Morrey suggested.

"I agree," said Sergio. "Add his two confederates to the list, Packie Erickson and Boyce Carsten. They think they are so well insulated behind their stooges that they'll never be detected, let alone prosecuted."

"What about that so-called financial adviser from Cheyenne who has been bilking our senior citizens and leaving them penniless?"

"You mean Fenton F. Dillman!" Toby responded. "We've been trying for over two years to nail that crook."

"He's one slippery eel," Sergio admitted. "He stays just inside the boundaries of the law, far enough to stay off law enforcements' radar."

"He'll slip up some day," promised Morrey. "They all do. He'll get careless thinking he'll never get caught. That's when we'll nail his ass."

"If my math is correct, that's eight of the top ten on the *hit list*," said Toby. "Surely there are two more we can add before we matriculate with the ladies and the children."

The ladies and children must have been feeling like widows and orphans, as several of them at that very moment descended on the study, making the circle of intimates feel guilty. They would have to wait another day to complete their top ten.

CHAPTER 3

A Slap in the Face

It was Christmastime, but the district attorney's office was not receiving any Christmas gifts from the Paraiso county commissioners. In fact, much to Morrey's dismay, the DA's budget for the upcoming year was decreased. It and the sheriff 's office were the only two county departments that were the victims of what had been tabbed the county's austerity program.

Both Morrey and Sergio were livid. Not only would they be prevented from adding much-needed staff, but they were in jeopardy of being unable to retain their current personnel. They could cut back on paper clips, photocopy products, and seminar expense, but not personnel. That was an unreasonable and unrealistic expectation. Their offices already were unable to compete with the lure of the private sector in the area of recruitment. That was a problem that would now be exacerbated by the commissioners' ill-conceived budget cut.

Morrey's peak annual salary as the district attorney was $65,000. His was one of the lowest paid in the state. His adjusted gross income for the tax year immediately prior to his assuming office had been more than twice that. That was almost seven years ago, and Morrey was seething. The budget cut was a slap in the face, an insult. The previous year, he had been cited as the outstanding district attorney for the state. Currently, he was the president-elect of the Colorado District Attorney's Association. He was touted as the best of the best, and yet he was one of the lowest paid district attorneys in the state. More than once Morrey toyed with the idea of returning to private practice. With his talents he could probably quadruple his income. However, the thought was always short-lived—his heart and soul were into seeing that justice was done, not just collecting paychecks or racking up convictions.

Sergio was not faring much better. He had been the sheriff of Paraiso County for over thirty years. His great-great-grandfather's brother had been the county's first sheriff. Sergio maintained a model law enforcement agency which was envied by his constituents and emulated by his fellow sheriffs. There was not another sheriff who could compare.

• • •

Because the district attorney's office was just down the hall from the county commissioners, it was the first to receive a copy of the new budget.

Even though Sergio was downstairs and one of the last to receive his department's budget, he was on the telephone first. "Morrey," he blasted, "the dispiteous county commissioners have for all intents and purposes eliminated the sheriff's department. They're trying to starve us to death and phase us out." Morrey visualized Sergio waving his copy of the budget in the air as he continued his rant. "What in hell's name are they afraid of? Why, the overpaid, overrated, and yes, overweight cowards can just…just… I'm on my way to tell them what they can do with my job."

"If you're headed that way now, please leave your service revolver in your desk drawer and stop by my office first," Morrey said sarcastically.

"Don't need my roscoe to deal with that bunch of wimps. See you in a few." Within less than a minute, so it seemed, he was in Morrey's office, flushed and ready to exterminate the commissioners and anyone else who got in the way.

"I suppose you got a ten percent cost of living increase for your staff, including the janitor, and a green light to add a dozen or so new prosecutors," he snorted.

"Double that," Morrey said sarcastically. With that, he closed his office door and locked it. He then ushered Sergio over to a small table, where he placed a bottle of Sergio's favorite, which he had removed from his lower desk drawer, and two glasses. Sergio did the honors.

As they clanked glasses, Sergio, now in a more subdued voice, said, "You know I can get in trouble over this."

"Too late," Morrey replied, "besides I won't tell if you won't."

They traded budgets. After their mutterings, shakes of the head, teeth clinching, lip biting, and rough treatment of the hapless sheets of paper comprising their respective budgets, they both just stared at each other. As their eyes met, rage turned into controlled anger, then into disbelief, and finally into what a therapist might describe as mental distress.

"Just because I left roscoe in my desk drawer doesn't mean that I've become compliant," said Sergio.

"Only means you've exercised good judgment and are in control of your senses," replied Morrey.

"You're supposed to be the chief law enforcement officer of the district," said Sergio. "And I'm supposed to be the chief law enforcement officer of the county. Appears both are only in name and job description. By controlling the purse strings, the county commissioners are in reality the chief law enforcement officers and gods of both the district and the county."

"Well put," replied Morrey. "It appears we're being manipulated by Doris Grey and Harriett Wensel, who being a majority, are the voice of the commissioners. Poor old Benjamin Cromwell literally is the odd man out. He'll do whatever Doris and Harriett tell him to do!"

"Madams Grey and Wensel, in case you haven't noticed, Morrey, are newbies; both have been residents here for less than five years."

"Medicinal purposes!" Morrey smiled as he poured them another round. Taking a sip from his glass, he resumed his seat behind his desk, and continued, "Sergio, what do you suppose Doris Grey, the high and mighty chairperson of the board of county commissioners, will do the next time hunters trespass on their ranch and she calls for assistance? What do you suppose she'll do when you say you don't have the manpower or that your budget doesn't allow it?"

"You know damn well she'll want my head on a platter and will start a recall campaign!" replied Sergio in disgust.

"Precisely. Maybe if the citizens are upset enough, the groundswell might just result in their being recalled or replaced at the polls."

"Recall would get rid of them pronto. Since their terms are somewhat staggered, Doris and Harriett won't have to run for reelection for another two and a half years, and poor old ineffective Ben only has six months left of his term."

"Recall is time-consuming, and it would take a lot of effort and expense to wage an effective battle. I know there are a lot of unhappy people out there, but organizing such a campaign would be a challenge. Still, there is more than one way to skin a cat."

"Morrey, that grin tells me there's something up your sleeve. Want to share?"

"Hell, yes!" said Morrey. "Remember the commissioners' secretary, Megan Frye, when she was fired last year? Well, she met with Toby shortly thereafter and blew the whistle, so to speak. She accused the commissioners of padding their expense accounts, using county vehicles for personal errands, making long-distance calls to relatives on county telephones, having her type personal letters and run personnel errands for them, and using the county computers for nefarious contacts. We thought her complaints to be like the fox's accusation in Aesop's fable—just a lot of sour grapes. Maybe we miscalculated."

Sergio raised his brows. Morrey now had

Sergio's complete attention. "Yes, I remember you telling me about it at the time. Taking public money or using public property for personal gain is a felony, correct?"

"Sergio, even if they took a postage stamp belonging to the county and stuck it on an envelope to mail a birthday card to one of their relatives, obviously without reimbursing the county, they would have committed embezzlement of public property. There's no threshold amount as in the theft statute. It can be just one penny. That's a felony, and guess what that felony would do? Among other things, it would disqualify them from holding public office! Savvy?"

"Bingo! We'd better start looking for three new commissioners and making reservations for the current band of thieves at the state pen."

"Not so fast, my man. Because of the apparent conflict of interest, we'd be wise to have a special prosecutor and a special investigator appointed. I'm not sure the district judge would do that. The judge may think we're on a witch hunt, and because of the budget squabble, may liken us to the fox in Aesop's fable."

Looking thoughtful, Sergio ran his finger around the rim of his glass making a squeaky sound. He finally said, "This is a slippery slope for your office, Morrey. What if the attempt fails? Then you're in a position far worse than what you're in now. Aren't you, in essence, cutting off your nose to spite your face? Adverse consequences could be dire, as you well know."

"I've considered that, my friend, and think I may have a solution. We've had a grand jury empaneled for quite some time now. We've used the grand jury sparingly, mainly to bypass preliminary hearings in sexual assault cases to keep the victims from having to testify and in some politically sensitive cases as well, but that's the extent. This is the type of case for which the grand jury has been created. Twelve citizens, tried and true, hear a complaint then decide whether or not a crime has been committed, and if so, whether it was committed by the accused. If they don't return an indictment, no one is the wiser. If they do, it will be their doing, and my office will then be obligated to prosecute."

"Bravo, you sly son-of-a-gun!" Sergio said while applauding. "You will only be doing what you are mandated by statute to do, nothing more, nothing less. Otherwise, you'll be violating your oath to uphold the law. Right?"

"Certainly, I have the duty to bring the matter to the grand jury's attention. When I become aware of a crime, even by public officials, I can't just turn my head or sweep it under the rug. In fact, if indeed the county commissioners or any of them commit a crime and I don't prosecute, I've committed a crime myself."

"Of course," Sergio commented, "but you don't even need the grand jury. You could file charges on your own."

"Yes," Morrey acknowledged, "but I'm sure if I filed that would be misconstrued and the rumor mill would have it that I was just being vindictive or abusing my power."

"Well!" Sergio said cynically.

"Hold it right there!" Morrey interrupted. "I may be perturbed by what the commissioners have done with our budgets and am predisposed to tell them they can take my job and shove it. But that having been said, I take my attorney's oath and the oath I took upon my election and reelection as DA very seriously. I know I talk big when I am disgusted and distressed, but I will not compromise my values. I would only be pursuing prosecution because it was warranted."

"That's one of the qualities I have always admired in you, Morrey. You wouldn't sell your soul for any price. I'm grateful to God for having you as a son-in-law. It's too bad the county commissioners are so short-sighted and haven't recognized your worth."

"Sergio, you've been like a father to me. Hearing you say that validates all those tough decisions I've made and makes me more determined than ever to do the right thing. Vindictiveness will not be the motivation in my exacting justice from the holier-than-thou county commissioners. Besides, first degree official misconduct makes it a crime in our state for a public servant, such as me, to commit an unauthorized act relating to his office with intent to maliciously cause harm to another."

The two agreed to sleep on it and meet again the following day when Toby was available. They were not prepared, however, for what awaited them in the following day's morning news. There were forces at work that not even they fully understood

CHAPTER 4

Erecting the Guillotine

Morrey was in the shower when Sergio called. Monique interrupted to announce that her father was on the telephone. The digital clock on the nightstand beside the bed registered 6:18. *Why is Sergio calling this early?* Morrey wondered.

"How come you're not at work today?" Sergio razzed. "Enjoying another day of sick leave?"

Morrey detected a jovial tone in Sergio's voice, a tone he hadn't heard in quite some time. *Has Sergio finally gone over the edge?* "What in heaven's name do you want at this ungodly hour?"

"Look at the letters to the editor in the morning paper," Sergio ordered, "and call me right back."

It must be divine providence or divine intervention, Morrey thought as he read the first letter to the editor. He read it through twice just to make sure he hadn't misread it. The letter written by Alfredo Maldinado, an old-time resident who didn't have a reputation for mincing words, read:

Dear Editor:
My wife and I have been residents of Paraiso County for over sixty years. We were both

*born here, as were our parents. Our children
were raised here. Never have I witnessed such
total disregard for the property rights and safety
of our citizens than under the current regime of our
ineffective county commissioners.*

*Yesterday, we read in the Las Cruces Gazette that
the Paraiso county commissioners had granted
a zoning variance for the erection of a halfway
house for sexual perpetrators on the county side
of the city boundary. Not only do a number of
families with children reside in the area, but it will
be in close proximity to the newly constructed
Clinton High School. It will be on the main road in
and out of Las Cruces.*

*Neither our neighbors nor my wife or I received
notice of a hearing on the variance, and it
seems that the dictatorial mindset of our county
commissioners is on destroying our community,
putting our children and the rest of us at risk, and
driving the law-abiding citizens out of Paraiso. If
that is their goal, they certainly have a running
start. If someone circulates a recall petition, we
would like to be the first to sign.*

/s/ Alfredo Maldinado

Sergio must have had his hand on the phone because Morrey had barely dialed Sergio's number when he was greeted by, "Well, what are you waiting for?"

"Uncanny, eh?" Morrey replied. "Guess you know who Toby interviews first."

"Indeed I do! Toby needs to interview Megan Frye, especially since she has an axe to grind. The current secretary, Sylvia Lancaster, might also be a valuable source, that is if she'll even talk to us."

"It would be pretty tricky to interview Sylvia. She won't appreciate being positioned between a rock and a hard place. She certainly would be fodder for the grand jury. Megan still hasn't filed the wrongful discharge action she has been threatening. She was cooperative when she was terminated; she should be cooperative now. I'll have Toby arrange for a follow-up interview."

"Since all the criminal conduct, if any, occurred in the city, the city police and not me will have jurisdiction." After a brief pause, Sergio asked, "By the way, are any of the alleged offenses barred by the statute of limitations?"

"Second-degree official misconduct, being a petty offense, has to be brought within six months after the act is committed or it's forever barred. Since embezzlement of public money or property is a felony, charges can be brought anytime within three years. We'll need to watch that closely, and that may be another reason why we may want to expedite the process."

"Absolutely! Call me when you get to your office."

• • •

Still in his topcoat and barely in the door, Morrey was talking to Sergio face-to-face. Sergio advised Morrey to sit down, as there was another surprise waiting. Sergio had just hung up the telephone with Shay Bisben, the attorney they had been talking about on Christmas day. Bisben said he had a summons to serve and wanted to make sure there was someone at the sheriff's department who could serve it on the three county commissioners at their meeting scheduled at the courthouse that morning. Bisben said he was representing Megan Frye on a wrongful discharge claim against the county and the board of county commissioners individually and in their official capacity. Bisben said he would be filing the complaint with the clerk of the district court promptly at 9:00 a.m. As soon as the clerk issued the summons, he would bring it down to the sheriff's department to have it served along with a copy of the complaint.

Morrey was speechless. *Maybe nice guys don't*

finish last after all, he thought. He had just barely received the offending budget and hadn't really had time to plot against the commissioners nor formulate a blueprint for his course of action, and already the commissioners were headed, excuse the pun, before the guillotine. He had to do nothing.

"You still there?" Sergio asked, snapping Morrey back to the present.

"I'm still here but it feels like I'm dreaming. Somebody up there must really like us," he told Sergio.

"We're going to have to jump on this horse and ride it for all it's worth," Sergio said sharply.

And ride it they did!

• • •

Morrey wasted no time when he found out about the documents to be served on the commissioners. He contacted Toby instructing him to call Shay Bisben and arrange to interview Shay's client. However, before Megan Frye would be interviewed, Bisben insisted that the district attorney's office grant her immunity on any of the matters she discussed. By implicating the commissioners, she didn't want to implicate herself. Not being able to prosecute her for her possible complicity was a fair trade—the commissioners' heads on a platter for hers. Without her testimony, they felt it would be difficult, if not impossible, to obtain a conviction against the most culpable.

With her attorney having obtained complete immunity and her attorney present, Megan, as the prosecution team later was heard to say, spilled her guts. Because Bisben had negotiated a ban on tape recorders, Toby wrote feverishly taking notes in his modified version of shorthand.

The prosecution team consisted mainly of Morrey, Toby, and assistant district attorney, Terrence Brockerton. They all took turns asking Megan questions. Megan was in her late twenties, trim, and attractive. She wore her long, blonde hair in a ponytail, and her fine features were dominated by sparkling greenish-blue eyes and a broad, engaging smile that would have made her dentist proud.

Megan would be the quintessential witness, the poster child for all would-be prosecution witnesses. She didn't equivocate, was forward and direct, and very articulate. It was obvious that she had taken speech classes and maybe even acting lessons. She was not at all timid and seemed to be at ease being the center of attention. She also proved to have a remarkable memory, one that the prosecution team hoped would make for a slam-dunk conviction. She was a first round draft choice without doubt, and the prosecution team was grateful she was on their side.

Although her demeanor was serious, Megan didn't appear to be nervous or anxious. For starters, she discussed the *modus operandi* of the commissioners upon Doris Grey's election as chairperson in indulging in unauthorized fringies. Within the twelve-month period immediately prior to her termination, Megan witnessed the following acts, which she described in great detail:

1. All three commissioners made repeated, private long distance calls on county telephones. It was not unusual for the commissioners to have her place the calls. The county was never reimbursed.

2. All three commissioners used county postage stamps for personal mailings They were always asking to *borrow* stamps to pay personal bills, send birthday, Christmas, and similar cards to loved ones, and for personal correspondence. Since she took the mail to the drop box at the post office each day, she sorted the mail and took notice of the addressees. The county was never reimbursed.

3. All three commissioners used the county photocopy machine to duplicate personal documents. She was sometimes asked to run the copies and unjam the machine from time to time retrieving the offending documents that she determined were for the most part of a personal nature. The county was never reimbursed.

4. All three commissioners used the county computers for their personal benefit. She watched as Doris and Harriett communicated with pen pals. Doris even bragged of having an affair over the Internet and was avoiding detection at home by using the county computers. Many of their personal letters were formalized on the county's word-processing equipment. She could always tell they were engaged in personal use of the word-processing equipment because normally only county matters were relegated to her. The county was never reimbursed for their personal use.

5. All three commissioners had used county vehicles from time to time to run personal errands. On one occasion, Harriet *borrowed* a county vehicle to attend a niece's wedding in Fort Collins because her vehicle was in the shop. Doris *borrowed* a county truck when she and her husband moved into their new home. In fact, all three used various pieces of county equipment for home and yard projects, and all borrowed the key to obtain fuel at the county gas pumps. She knew for certain that each had their personal vehicles serviced at the county garage. To her knowledge, the county was never reimbursed.

6. All three commissioners stayed extra days in Orlando while attending a national county commissioners convention. The county picked up the hotel, restaurant, and transportation expenses for those extra days as well as for their respective spouses. She knew because she was familiar with their itinerary and was the one who processed their vouchers. The county was never reimbursed.

7. Doris and Harriett had submitted mileage vouchers for nonexistent travel. She knew because on several occasions when the two claimed to have been traveling, they were actually in their offices in the courthouse. When Doris became chairperson, they changed the reimbursement process for meals. Instead of providing vouchers backed by receipts, they devised a meal allotment figure for each of the various meals that required no receipts and to which they were entitled even if they incurred no expense. She knew because she was present when the two discussed the *per diem* spin-off benefits to them personally.

8. The three regularly invaded the county's petty cash drawer to purchase pastries and coffee or have her do it for them She remembered several times when the commissioners summoned her to bring in money from the petty cash drawer to pay local vendors who were peddling candy and other snacks. The county was never reimbursed.

9. Doris and Harriett, shortly before Megan was terminated, had home security systems installed in their homes at county expense ostensibly to ensure their safety. As far as she knew, the county was still paying the monthly fees.

10. All three of the commissioners were provided county cell phones that were to be used for county business but were used primarily by the commissioners for personal calls, both local and long distance. She knew because she had heard them discuss it. At least during the time she was there, the county was never reimbursed.

Megan was then asked if she had read the letter to the editor in the *Las Cruces Gazette* regarding the zoning variance granted to the group intending to build the halfway house for sexual perpetrators. She said she had and personally knew the letter's writer, Alfredo Maldinado. She said, however, she didn't know anything about the proposed project. She said she couldn't help there but remembered the commissioners granting a controversial zoning request to a developer who had several months before invited the commissioners to a ski holiday in Aspen. She stated Doris and Harriett took him up on the offer, and they and their respective spouses were guests at the developer's condominium. Ben, who had not gone on the excursion, voted against the zoning request. When asked how long ago that was, she responded, "approximately two years ago."

When asked about whether the previously enumerated acts were committed within the last three years, she replied yes and stated that they, for the most part, were ongoing. She inquired why they asked. Morrey explained that the statute of limitations required that charges on felonies be brought within three years, eighteen months for misdemeanors and six months for petty offenses. If charges were not brought within those respective time periods, he explained, they were forever barred.

Megan appeared surprised and disappointed to learn that the impropriety with regard to accepting a gratuity in exchange for the granting of the zoning request, though a crime, was barred by the statute of limitations inasmuch as it would be considered either a first or second degree official misconduct, the former being a misdemeanor and the latter a petty offense. She stated she was relieved to learn, however, that the other acts of impropriety for the most part were felonies and not barred by the statute of limitations

"Not only does it appear that most of the criminal acts you enumerated are felonies, specifically embezzlement of public property," said Morrey, "but collectively, they establish a pattern of criminality or pattern of racketeering under the Colorado Organized Crime Control Act (COCCA), the counterpart of the federal RICO statute. Under the Colorado statute, a violation of COCCA is a high-level felony. In other words, it's a serious offense and carries with it the same penalty as for second-degree murder. The period in which such an action must be brought is three years."

Squinting and tilting her head, Megan asked, "So by just stealing a postage stamp from the county, the commissioners committed a felony? And by committing that act and the other acts repeatedly over a period of time, that constituted a pattern of racketeering, a serious felony?"

"Exactly," Morrey responded. "If the commissioners are convicted of a series of crimes, the sentences could run consecutively—that is, one sentence stacked on top of another. A COCCA conviction alone carries a penalty of from eight to twenty-four years in the Colorado State Penitentiary as well as a hefty fine and surcharge."

"Unbelievable!" Megan exclaimed shaking her head. "What about my role in all of this? If I hadn't been granted immunity, would I be charged with felonies as well?"

"To answer that succinctly," Morrey responded, "you would be deemed to be a complicitor. If you were found to have aided, abetted, assisted, or encouraged the perpetration of those offenses you would be just as criminally responsible as the commissioners. Shay did you a huge service in obtaining, in your behalf, immunity from prosecution."

"Whew!" Megan exclaimed gritting her teeth. "I guess I had no idea I could get in trouble by just following orders. What if none of us knew that what we were doing was a crime?"

Terrence Brockerton fielded that question. "Ignorance of the law is no excuse," he said. "Whether you knew or didn't know is immaterial."

"Of course," Megan admitted, "I knew what the commissioners were doing was improper, but I didn't think that what I was doing was improper and certainly not a crime. When I questioned their practices, they were somewhat irate and accused me of being insubordinate. On one occasion, after a particularly heated confrontation, Doris showed me the door and told me that if I didn't like what was going on, I should quit. In fact, it was not long after that incident that she told me to clean out my desk and return my key."

"In retrospect," Shay said, putting words in Megan's mouth, "if you knew what you know now, you would have probably resigned a long time ago."

"Being the loyal and devoted employee I was, and for the most part liking my job, I turned my head and closed my eyes on a lot of the commissioners' shenanigans. I guess I looked up to the commissioners and felt their judgment was beyond the misgivings and challenge of a mere mortal like me."

"You're not the first and won't be the last to feel that way," said Toby.

Megan, through her legal mouthpiece, agreed to cooperate in the prosecution of the commissioners and to testify before the grand jury in the event that was the direction the district attorney's office would go. Megan also agreed to keep everything hush-hush.

Before dispersing, each camp agreed to keep the other camp advised of any significant developments. In the interim, Megan would search her memory for anything else that would aid in the prosecution and so inform her attorney who, in turn, would so inform the district attorney's office. From each of their perspectives, the meeting was a resounding success and their expectations optimistic.

LICENSE TO CONVICT — CARROLL MULTZ

CHAPTER 5

Impaneling a Grand Jury

The grand jury has sometimes been likened by its detractors to a Star Chamber reminiscent of the oppressive, secret nonjury proceedings of the English courts in the 1600s that were marked by forced confessions and arbitrary decisions. Although the grand jury operates in secrecy, the similarities stop there.

The Paraiso County grand jury rotated jurors on a calendar year basis. The grand jury for the ensuing calendar year was selected in December and was sworn in on the first Monday of the following January. The chief district court judge and the district attorney jointly determine who will sit. Those selected for the current year, as in the past, consisted mainly of longtime citizens of Paraiso county. No newbies on this grand jury.

The grand jury differs from a trial jury in that the grand jury's role is not to determine whether an accused is guilty or not guilty but rather whether there is probable cause or reasonable grounds to believe a crime has been committed, and if so, whether the person being investigated committed it.

If the grand jury determines that there *is* probable cause, they return what is called a *true bill* and file with the court a charge form called an *indictment*. If the grand jury does not find probable cause, it returns a *no-true bill*.

In the absence of a grand jury, it is within the sole discretion of the district attorney as to whether criminal charges will be filed. In such cases, a charged accused, depending on the classification of the crime, is entitled to a preliminary hearing. At a preliminary hearing, it is the presiding judge who determines whether there is probable cause. If there is no finding of probable cause, the case is dismissed; otherwise, it is set to proceed through the criminal justice process. With an indictment, however, the accused is not entitled to a preliminary hearing.

• • •

Because of the political connotations and ramifications and perceived conflict of interest, Morrey opted *not* to file charges against the Paraiso County commissioners but to have the case presented to and filtered through a grand jury. Because of the dilemma in prosecuting the officials who set his budget and his perceived bias, he also opted to ask the chief district judge, Pinkerton T. Calloway, to appoint a special prosecutor to present the case to the grand jury and a special investigator to assist.

The grand jury, through the courts, has the power to subpoena persons and records. All persons, however, have a constitutional right to refuse to testify or produce records if it might tend to incriminate them. If they receive immunity, such as Megan Frye, they cannot hide behind that shield and will be required to testify.

It was anticipated that Doris Grey, Harriett Wensel, and Benjamin Cromwell, upon receiving subpoenas, would be invoking their Fifth Amendment privilege—especially after they had conferred with an attorney.

Since the proceedings are secret, what goes on in the session stays in the session. Only after an accused is indicted does he or she have the right to obtain a transcript of the proceedings involving his or her case. Also, only one witness is allowed to be present in the session at any one time, and after a witness has testified, he or she is not allowed to relate his or her testimony to anyone else. When all the evidence has been concluded with reference to the particular matter, the grand jury retires to make its probable cause determination in private. The grand jury depends on the prosecuting attorney to inform and guide it on the law and in the preparation of the charge form or any other needed documents or pleadings.

Morrey didn't need to play all his cards and had several aces up his sleeve. One was his option to file charges against the commissioners even if the grand jury returned a no-true bill. Also, the impaneling of the grand jury was a win-win situation—especially with the appointment of a special prosecutor and special investigator. Nothing that happened in or emanated from the grand jury would be perceived as his doing. Morrey wondered if maybe he was taking the chicken way out. He then rationalized that if by some quirk of fate the grand jury didn't return a true-bill, he would be making the prosecutorial decision.

• • •

Morrey succeeded in having Judge Calloway appoint Gilman "Gil" Vedder as a special prosecutor and Perry Simms as a special investigator of the newly impaneled grand jury. Gil was the assistant district attorney from another district across the state, and Perry was Gil's investigator. Morrey knew both through the Colorado District Attorney's Association. They would now be the dominant forces in the drama that would unfold before the Paraiso County grand jury.

• • •

On that cold overcast last Monday of January, Morrey showed Gil and Perry the spare office that had just been cleared of closed files, outdated law books, and other clutter, an office that would be their exclusive domain for an indeterminable period of time.

Toby met in his office with Perry, and there Toby briefed Perry on the nature of the commissioner investigation. Simultaneously, Gil met with Morrey in the DA's conference room. As soon as Terrence Brockerton returned from court, he would be joining his boss and the newly appointed special prosecutor.

Knowing that Shay Bisben had migrated from Gil's home district and Shay being the attorney for the key witness in the grand jury probe of the errant county commissioners, Morrey asked Gil if he knew Shay.

"Are you kidding?" Gil responded. "I grew up with Shay's daddy. Unfortunately, I was involved in the prosecution of a drug bust that resulted in Shay's arrest. I'm not supposed to talk about it because Shay successfully completed his deferred judgment and sentence. No conviction was entered, and his record was completely erased. He was a newly admitted attorney at the time, and a felony would have taken his license."

"As it is, I'm sure that not even his arrest appears on his record. By the way, Gil, what kind of drugs was he messed up in?"

"Just marijuana, and it involved only a small amount. Now it would be only a misdemeanor, but in those days, possession of any amount was a felony. We were giving a lot of deferred judgments and sentences back then. If the offender cleaned up his act, got professional help, performed community service, and otherwise complied with all of the conditions imposed by the court, he got a bye. Otherwise, he would end up with a felony conviction, and in Shay's case, loss of his license to practice law."

"I guess my advice to those who flaunt the law is: If you don't want to lose your license to practice law, then don't commit a felony!" Morrey said unsympathetically as Terrence Brockerton entered the room. Soon they were joined by Toby and Perry.

In a few hours, the prosecution team, as they would become known, began constructing the framework upon which they would build in the grand jury's probe of the errant county commissioners. The allegations were treated as just that and would have to be substantiated in order to unleash the awesome power of the beast they called the *grand jury*. Once turned loose, however, there would be no turning back.

• • •

At lunch, when Gil ordered a double martini, no one said anything. When he ordered his second, Morrey glared at Terrence, careful not to be noticed by Gil. But when Gil ordered still a third, Morrey, Terrence, and Toby wondered if maybe they had made a serious error in judgment. They also wondered if Gil's recent divorce may have been the result of his drinking or just the reverse—his drinking the result of his recent divorce.

Upon return from lunch, the prosecution team was met by Shay Bisben and Megan Frye. Shay had not been warned that Gil Vedder had been appointed special prosecutor. Morrey wasn't sure how Gil would be perceived, since Gil had been the prosecutor on Shay's personal drug case. Having agreed to a deferred judgment and sentence, however, Morrey was fairly certain Gil would be embraced as Shay's savior. And that's exactly what Shay's reaction was upon seeing Gil. Shay apparently hadn't forgotten the man who had rescued him from certain disaster early in his career and his eyes, meeting Gil apparently for the first time since, conveyed his deep respect and heartfelt gratitude.

It was a rare occurrence to investigate a county commissioner, let alone three of them! So that Gil didn't end up with egg on his face, he was eager to interview the whistleblower. Although Morrey had boasted of the prowess of the informant, Gil wanted to judge for himself. Because Morrey and his staff would continue to be involved in the criminal investigation and would, in all likelihood, be the ones prosecuting the case at trial in the event of an indictment, Morrey, Terrence, and Toby would be present when Gil interviewed Megan.

It started out as a get-acquainted session, but it was not long before Gil was asking the tough questions. It was difficult to determine if Gil was driven by skepticism or thoroughness, but he probed deeply into Megan's personal knowledge of the purported events as well as her motive for coming forward with information that would make her vulnerable to possible public scorn and ridicule.

"It may be perceived by some," Gil said to Megan, "that you have an axe to grind in light of your recent termination. Retaliation would be a natural tendency."

Megan suddenly became defensive and at a loss for words. It was obvious she could be rattled and fodder for a seasoned cross-examiner. Judging from Shay's reaction, this was a side of which not even he was aware.

"I—I—," Megan stammered, "am not a spiteful person. In fact, I'm just the opposite. I'm only coming forward … because it is the right thing to do." Megan's eyes watered, and her lips quivered. She hastily retrieved a tissue from her purse and began dabbing at the tears.

Megan briskly pushed Shay aside when he tried to console her. "I'm … m … okay," she muttered. "I'm just very sensitive about this whole thing. At one time I was engaged to Doris' son."

Without giving Megan time to compose herself, Gil impulsively asked, "Who broke off the engagement?"

"He did," Megan snapped back and continued to sob.

The prosecution team looked at each other as if to say, *We should've known it was too good to be true. Megan is anything but a disinterested witness. Without corroboration, our prosecution no doubt is compromised.*

• • •

The prosecution team was afraid that the commissioners might purge the records once they caught wind of the probe. Surely with the commissioners' offices being just around the corner, they or their eyes and ears would know of the comings and goings of the informant, who the commissioners no doubt in short order, would be referring to among themselves as the traitor. Because of the budgetary ramifications and being the dispenser of the county funds, the commissioners obviously were aware of the empanelment of the county grand jury and Judge Calloway's appointment of the special prosecutor and the special investigator. Hopefully, they didn't know yet that they were the ones being investigated.

Although normally the prosecution team would have a subpoena served on Sylvia Lancaster, Megan's replacement, they were afraid that what the grand jury would be seeking would just mysteriously disappear. To avoid that, they would need a search warrant and the sooner the better. Once they did that, however, the cat would defiantly be out of the bag. The commissioners then would know for certain they were the target of the grand jury probe.

• • •

When they arrived at the assigned courtroom shortly after 6:30 p.m., over half of the grand jurors were already sitting in the partially lit, now otherwise vacant, courtroom. The all-familiar courtroom would be the venue for this and all future grand jury proceedings. After turning on all the lights and repositioning the counsel tables to accommodate the big five and all their legal paraphernalia, Brooke Sorrell, a certified freelance court reporter assigned to the grand jury by Judge Calloway, arrived.

Brooke was known to Morrey, Terrence, and Toby and was introduced to Gil and Perry. She had already received strict instructions from Judge Calloway that she was to be present at all grand jury sessions; was to report on all grand jury proceedings and testimony from commencement to adjournment; was to preserve and file with Judge Calloway any reporter's notes or transcripts; and was not to release or destroy any notes or transcripts without prior court approval.

Brooke was young and pleasant to look at, and as Gil would later remark, a scintillating diversion from the females on the grand jury. She was told it would be the foreman and not her who would administer the oath and swear in the witnesses who would be testifying before the grand jury. She appeared obsequious and open to Gil's suggestions. She would be a welcomed addition to the Paraiso County grand jury proceeding.

As the clock on the four-sided courthouse tower struck seven, Morrey instructed the grand jurors to be seated. Mainly by design, they were long-time residents of Paraiso County. There were seven men and five women, with an average age of fifty-seven. They came from various walks of life, and there was a relatively even mix of race, color, and creed. All previously had indicated their desire to serve and appeared eager to do so.

While Brooke tickled the keys on her stenographic machine, Morrey introduced the participants and commenced his canned opening remarks followed by Grand Jury 101. The grand jury was provided with a roadmap. He alerted the grand jury as to the nature of the first matter to be presented and then relegated the podium to Gil. Gil then revealed the general nature of the investigation of the three Paraiso county commissioners.

Not one of the grand jurors reacted, at least not that was discernable, which somewhat surprised Morrey, Terrence, and Toby. The grand jurors appeared unabashed by the revelation and remained stoic as Gil outlined what to expect that coming Thursday and Friday. The grand jury authorized their foreman to assist in obtaining the requisite subpoenas from the court.

• • •

Armed with a search warrant, Hunter Thorpe and Quavos Sandoval, both from the Las Cruces Police Department, accompanied by the grand jury's special investigator, Perry Simms, descended upon the offices of the Paraiso county commissioners. They were soon joined by Gil Vedder and Griff Remington, the chief of police. Sylvia Lancaster, the current secretary for the commissioners, was the only one present when they arrived. Sylvia was a dowdy middle-aged woman who was more than cooperative in assisting. Polite and compliant, she made the investigators' job relatively easy and productive.

Two computers were accessed, with Sylvia's help, and examined and seized. In the interim, numerous boxes of records, journals, vouchers, receipts, billing statements, and the like were carted off to a police van and later transported to the police department. Theoretically, most of the records they seized would have been available under the state's version of the Freedom of Information Act. However, with an investigation looming, it was uncertain how much would have been restricted from private examination and duplication and how much would have just mysteriously disappeared or claimed to have never existed.

In less than two hours, the search and resulting seizures were completed. Just as Chief Remington was handing a receipt itemizing all the items seized to Sylvia, Benjamin Cromwell appeared on the scene. The commissioners would all now know that something was awry. And after they quizzed Sylvia, they would be putting two and two together. Maybe they already had connected the dots.

Quavos Sandavol was the police department's IT whiz. He had within relatively quick order found personal e-mails from Doris and Harriett and uncovered Doris' Internet affair with an Irving Snowden in Lancaster, England. Officer Thorp was having similar success in tracing the long-distance telephone calls itemized on Mountain Bell's county billing statements for the last three years. At least several dozen calls were placed to a number in Lancaster, England, all listed to the aforementioned Irving Snowden. It was deemed unnecessary, at least for the moment, to issue a subpoena to Mountain Bell for production of the toll records. The investigators, for the most part, already had the information they needed.

Officer Thorp had stopped by the county shop and examined the records for sign-ins and sign-outs of county vehicles for the past three years and obtained copies of those containing the names of the county commissioners. He also obtained from the shop foreman, Carlos Castilla, copies of various schedules of fuel withdrawals from the county pumps with accompanying signatures. He would be cross-checking to see which ones corresponded to county business and which ones didn't. The commissioners' master calendar for each of the past three years would be helpful in that regard. As with car rentals, the shop records reflected the beginning and ending mileage for all county vehicles that were checked out by county officials and/or employees. He would be cross-referencing those as well.

Before day's end, Perry had met with Jayden Greene of Greene's Security Service, Inc., and obtained copies of the security contracts for the security systems installed in Doris Grey's and Harriett Wensel's residences. The contracts were signed by the two in their individual capacities. However, the two accounts were set up so that the county was billed for and paid the installation costs as well as the succeeding monthly service fees. Perry found in checking with Officer Thorpe that among the items seized from the commissioners' office were billing records that confirmed the above.

Perry's assignment also included checking the calls on each of the commissioners' county-issued cell phones. Because of the privacy restrictions, to do so required considerable red tape. It was ultimately determined, however, that there was a flat fee paid each month by the county, and personal calls in no way impacted the amount of such required payment. *No harm, no foul!* In checking with Gil, it was determined that personal use of the county cell phones probably didn't rise to the level of a venial sin let alone a mortal sin, and maybe no sin at all. Gil said filing charges on something that petty would only dilute the seriousness of the other offenses.

In the process of the investigation, it was discovered that Ben was the only commissioner to execute a bond conditioned upon him faithfully and honestly discharging the duties of his office as required by law. Neither Doris nor Harriett had executed such a bond. That was confirmed in checking the records of the county clerk and recorder's office, where the bond was required to be filed. Even though failure to do so was only a misdemeanor, the penalty was a rather hefty fine and imprisonment in the county jail for not less than thirty days or more than six months. Gil wondered what impact the fines would have on Megan's civil action in the event the two were determined to be judgment proof.

It also appeared that the commissioners had held meetings in violation of a Colorado statute sometimes referred to as the Sunshine Act that required the board of county commissioners to meet in open session and allow all persons to attend.

The commissioners had conducted a number of special meetings other than legitimate executive sessions, whereby the public was wrongfully excluded. The penalty for such offense, however, was a minimum fine. It was really Gil's call as to whether he wanted to lob pellets when he had so many grenades in his arsenal.

The big bomb in Gil's arsenal was dependent on whether the commissioners knowingly received proceeds derived from a pattern of racketeering activity (i.e., engaged in two or more acts of racketeering activity that posed a sufficient threat of continuity, having the same or similar purposes, results, participants, victims, or methods of commission and were otherwise interrelated). If they did, then they would be deemed to have committed a serious felony punishable by imprisonment in the state penitentiary for not less than eight nor more than twenty-four years. By violating the Colorado Organized Crime Control Act (COCCA), they would also be subjected to a hefty surcharge.

In no time, Gil and Perry were able to do the math and come to the same conclusion as Morrey, Terrence, and Toby. There were indeed multiple or repeated acts of criminality in each of the categories they investigated. And there were multiple categories. The acts of criminality were committed over a long period of time. They persisted up to the current date and would likely have continued well into the future had it not been for acts beyond their control, namely: the disruption caused by the investigation in progress. The offenses were similar, if not identical, in purposes, results, participants, victims, and methods of commission. If they were not interrelated, then Cain and Able had not been related or interrelated, nor had Sonny and Cher.

Gil had enough to obtain multiple count indictments consisting of mainly felonies. And it was difficult to predict what other bugs might emerge from the woodwork as the investigation unfolded and the complainants came forward. In letter and spirit, the Board of County Commissioners of Paraiso County had certainly violated their oath of office to support the constitutions of the United States and the State of Colorado and to perform the duties of their office to the best of their ability.

Gil was eager for Perry to interview the county clerk and recorder of Paraiso County who, by statute, was designated as the clerk of the board of county commissioners. Since the clerk's signature or facsimile was required on all checks and authorizations for disbursement, it would be probative to determine if her stamped signature thereon was authorized. Also, the clerk was required to record all of the board's proceedings, record all votes, and sign all orders issued by the board for the payment of money.

Fanana Sosa was one of the most popular and respected of the county's elected officials. As the Paraiso county clerk and recorder, and therefore clerk of the board, it was expected she would be able to provide some of the missing pieces. Gil and Perry would also be interviewing the county treasurer and others.

• • •

Mammoth headlines in the *Las Cruces Gazette* that frigid January Wednesday morning announced for the world to see: ***COMMISSIONERS' OFFICE RAIDED.*** The subheading read: ***Police Seize County Records***. In the center of the article was a photograph of Commissioner Cromwell with a contrived shrug. *The Gazette* did a decent job of covering the *where, when,* and *how* of the raid but admitted they didn't know the *why.* Morrey speculated that the Megans of the world would be able to provide that answer.

The phones at the district attorney's office were ringing off the hook, and Gil and Perry were kept busy fielding questions, comments, and information from the newly informed. Many wanted to schedule appointments to meet with the two. At the head of the list was Alfredo Maldinado. He was still seething over the neighborhood halfway house fiasco and wanted the commissioners' heads delivered on a platter. A lot of the callers appeared paranoid, and Gil wondered if there were other whistleblowers out there who would be more than willing to trade information for immunity. Particularly suspicious was the call from a real-estate developer by the name of Beraldo Mingo. The big five speculated that Beraldo might be the one who owned the condominium in Aspen and was anxious not to want his gracious gesture of appreciation to be construed as a bribe.

• • •

Gil and Perry were now preoccupied with preparing the blueprint of the commissioner investigation to present to the grand jury on Thursday. It was anticipated that Megan's testimony and identification of various exhibits recently obtained would take up the better part of Thursday and likely Friday. The remainder of this day would be spent meeting with Megan and Shay in polishing Megan's anticipated testimony.

CHAPTER 6

The Day of Reckoning

Ever since the article had appeared in the newspaper, the bugs had been emerging from the woodwork. With all the detractors, the prosecution team was wondering how the commissioners were ever elected in the first place. The question now was not whether there would be enough fodder for the grand jury to find probable cause, but whether it would be overkill.

Today would be the first of many days the investigation of the errant county commissioners would be presented to the grand jury. Megan Frye would be the leadoff batter. She would tell what she knew mainly from her own personal knowledge. Although at trial she would be restricted from testifying as to hearsay statements (other than those emanating from the commissioners themselves), she would not be so constrained before the grand jury. Desmond Simmons, Hunter Thorpe, and Quavos Sandoval would testify as to their seizure of the journals, accounting sheets, documents, and other incriminating evidence relevant to their investigation.

The county shop foreman, Carlos Costilla, and the current secretary for the commissioners, Sylvia Lancaster, had been subpoenaed for late Friday afternoon just in case they could be accommodated. Carlos had been served with a subpoena and was expected to bring with him records substantiating the commissioners' unauthorized use of county vehicles, their requisitioning of fuel for their personal vehicles, and recently determined, their conscription of county employees using county vehicles and equipment to pave the commissioners' private lanes and driveways, and as recent as the past week, remove snow therefrom. Old Ben, it appeared, had partaken of this forbidden fruit along with his sister commissioners, and even though he was more guilty of stupidity than criminality, the big five would still be making reservations for him in the Colorado State Penitentiary in Canon City.

The blueprint of the investigation of the errant commissioners was laid before the grand jury in surprising detail. Even though the grand jury was an investigative body and the proceedings were structured as such, Gil's presentation resembled that of the prosecution's opening statement at trial. Gil, however, was careful not to invade the grand jury's province by suggesting one way or another as to whether indictments should be returned.

Before the presentation of any evidence, Gil reminded the grand jurors that the grand jury was an investigative body, and all the proceedings would be secret. Although he or Morrey could disclose the general purpose of the grand jury's investigation to the public, everyone else, including them, was precluded from making public disclosure until such time as indictments were returned. They were reminded of their oath of secrecy and advised that witnesses who appeared before them would be administered the same oath of secrecy in addition to the usual oath to tell the truth.

When one of the grand jurors raised her hand and asked Gil to explain once again the justification for secrecy, Gil repeated the litany: "To prevent the escape of those whose indictment may be contemplated; to prevent disclosure of derogatory information presented against someone who has not been indicted; to encourage witnesses to appear and speak freely; and to encourage grand jurors uninhibited investigation of and deliberation on suspected criminal activity."

Thinking it advisable to repeat, Gil stated, "Remember, any witness you subpoena to appear and testify or produce books, papers, documents, or other objects or items shall be entitled to have his or her attorney present. Although he or she may confer with his or her attorney, the attorney cannot be disruptive or make objections, arguments, or otherwise address you. By the way, the attorney is also required to take the oath of secrecy."

Gil continued, "After a witness has testified, he or she may be able to obtain a copy of his or her testimony, but only if authorized by court order. And remember, an indicted defendant will be able, with Judge Calloway's consent, to obtain all grand jury testimony and examine all tangible evidence relative to his or her case."

• • •

Megan Frye was called as Gil's first witness. She maintained her air of confidence as she entered the courtroom along with her attorney, Shay Bisben. The grand jury foreman, Benaventa Acapula, administered the oath.

Even under the circumstances, Megan emitted an ingratiating manner and ready smile that lit up the courtroom. Her job would be easy; all she had to do was tell the truth. In that moment of hush and solemnity, with the grand jurors poised in respectful anticipation, Megan kicked off an investigative journey that would ultimately change the course of Paraiso County history.

Megan would testify three more times over the next eight weeks. Sixteen other witnesses comprised of police officers, county personnel, Beraldo Mingo, and Jayden Greene would also be called to testify and supply the various links in the chain of criminality needed to indict.

Although Doris Grey, Harriett Wensel, and Benjamin Cromwell were subpoenaed to testify before the grand jury, they in essence by invoking their Fifth Amendment rights and upon advice of their respective attorneys, declined to answer any questions other than their names. They even refused to give their home addresses. Gil wondered how their lack of cooperation would set with the jury. After all, they were part of the county government being investigated, and trying to evade the issue by refusing to answer even the simple non-incriminating questions, made them look all the more guilty.

• • •

With the backup testimony, minutes of meetings, telephone toll records, vouchers, sign in/sign out sheets, cancelled checks, court records, bank records, journals, documents, computers, and the multiple count indictments, the foreman of the grand jury appeared in open court. The date: April 1, officially April Fool's Day. *How appropriate!*

The indictments against Doris Grey and Harriett Wensel were inconceivable. With over one hundred counts, the charge form was the size of a small telephone directory. The possible years of imprisonment exceeded three centuries and the possible fines exceeded twelve million dollars. Benjamin Cromwell, on the other hand was facing prosecution on *only* eighty counts. The possible penalties upon conviction were also mind boggling.

Felony warrants were issued by Judge Calloway, and the now indicted commissioners were allowed to turn themselves in. Bonds were set at $750,000 each for Grey and Wensel, and $500,000 for Cromwell. All three of the indicted posted surety bonds. After they were fingerprinted and their mug shots taken, they were released. With photographers shooting and television cameras rolling, the three shielded their faces with their hands and turned up collars as they were whisked away by family members to waiting cars that would transport them to their respective homes, where they would be spending only limited time in the ensuing years.

Each of the indicted hired attorneys from outside the Las Cruces area. All were high-profile attorneys. Gil began to wonder where all the money was coming from to pay their fees. None of the indicted had much money when first elected and had to borrow to pay their campaign expenses. Multiplying the loaves and fishes paled in comparison considering what the three had been able to do with their measly $17,500 annual salaries. The county had been kind to them, but not wittingly.

● ● ●

When it was time to say good-bye, it was not as easy as one might have expected. Gil and Perry had fought the good fight, and now they were passing the baton on to Morrey, Terrance, and Toby to prosecute the cases to a resolution.

"Are you sure you don't want Perry and me to ride this horse to the finish line?" Gil asked in an enthusiastic tone. "That way, you wouldn't have to dodge the inevitable scourge of the commissioner faithful and be the target of their wrath."

"I discussed that with Terrance and Toby," Morrey responded. "It certainly minimizes the political fall-out and is very tempting. However, it reminds me of two of my childhood playmates who lived down in the next block. Jerrold would pick the fight and leave Jarred, his twin brother, to finish it. The problem was that Jarred was not always at Jerrold's side, and there was always a day of reckoning."

It was obvious Gil and Perry were reluctant to leave. "I guess we've just had too much fun here," Perry said somberly. "We hate to leave you three to fend for yourselves. Unlike Morrey's friend Jarred, we'll be there if you need us."

Morrey, Terrance, and Toby realized that the ball was now in their court, and if the prosecution failed, it wouldn't be the fault of Gil and Perry.

• • •

Grey had hired the infamous Wellington D. Mitford from Boulder. He was the Harry Houdini of white and blue collar criminal defense. Only the rich and famous had been able to afford Mitford. Wensel hired Stanley R. Wiseman of Denver, and Cromwell hired Tanya Bennett-Correlli of Fort Collins. All three defense attorneys had been schooled in various district attorneys' offices around the state, and Bennett-Correlli had just recently resigned from the United States Attorney's Office, where she prosecuted complex computer fraud cases. They all came to the case of the errant county commissioners with a lot of notches on their belts.

Mitford, Wiseman, and Bennett-Correlli would no doubt be coordinating their efforts. However, among the egocentric college of defense attorneys, of which each was a card-carrying member, they would be careful, even among themselves, not to divulge the exact nature of their secret potion. The *coup de grace* that would herald the successful defense of his or her client's case would be unveiled only at that perfect moment and only as part of his or her sneak attack or surprise strategy. The defense attorney's humility was exceeded only by his or her brilliance.

Since the issues in the three prosecutions were merged and the evidence would be identical, at least as far as the sister county commissioners were concerned, Morrey was considering moving for a consolidation or merger of the three cases. If consolidation was opposed, old Ben would probably succeed, since he had fewer counts. Morrey wasn't sure what Judge Calloway would do with respect to the two women. Since they were in *pari delicto*, so to speak, he felt sure that at least those two cases would be consolidated. It would cut the work in his office substantially and save the taxpayers a considerable amount of money. He would first determine whether the cases were even contested. The three had been caught with their hands in the proverbial cookie jar, and they were covered with crumbs from head to toe. There didn't appear to be much wiggle room for any of the three.

Mitford, Wiseman, and Bennett-Correlli reminded the prosecution team of Genghis Khan, Julius Caesar, and Joan of Arc, respectively. They came to conquer. However, their attempt at establishing a foothold and instilling fear and intimidation failed miserably. They did succeed in obtaining copies of the grand jury transcripts and other discovery. However, all their other motions, including their motion to quash the indictments, were denied.

Wiseman and Bennett-Correlli, in behalf of their respective clients, Wensel and Cromwell, came to Morrey with hat in hand and on bended knee begging for a plea bargain. Mitford, on the other hand, with a poker face, attempted to bluff his way to a concession. Arrogance ultimately gave way to discretion, and Mitford ultimately was brought to his knees. He was not used to being in a beggar's role, but like Morrey had recently realized, "You can't win them all."

"I hope you don't think I'm coming from a position of weakness," Mitford had said. "I've never been one for playing games or wasting everyone's time or especially my client's money. And being a realist and knowing that the odds are stacked against my client, I don't see how it benefits anyone to prolong the agony. I could roll the dice and maybe obtain an acquittal, which is not beyond the bounds of possibility," said Mitford arrogantly. "But the downside would be just as dramatic. I'd be willing to discuss a plea to an allayed or reduced charge."

All of Mitford's rhetoric and pretense was for

naught, as Morrey understood only too well that Mitford was throwing in the towel and waving the proverbial white flag. Morrey's adversary did little to camouflage his desperation.

It was agreed that Grey and Wensel would each plead guilty to the COCCA charge and one embezzlement charge. Each would receive a twelve-year sentence and pay a fine of $25,000. Each would submit her resignation, effective immediately. Grey and Wensel would commence their time at the Women's Correctional Facility at Lyman, Colorado, and with an allowance for goodtime/earned time would be eligible for parole in less than six years.

Cromwell, on the other hand, was allowed to plead guilty to two embezzlement charges for which he received a two-year sentence and a $10,000 fine. Because of health problems and advanced years, he was placed under house arrest. He, too, would submit his resignation. He would conclude his years of public service in public disgrace. He, however, would not complete his sentence. Less than six weeks after being fitted with an ankle bracelet, he failed to awaken from his sleep.

A vacancy committee of the same political party as the vacating commissioners appointed three replacements who would hold office until the next general election. One of the new appointees was Milton Kincaid, Toby's father. All three would weather their respective elections and ably serve their allotted terms.

CHAPTER 7

Trial By Ordeal

Morrey was applauded for vindicating the dignity of the community. It was David versus Goliath. Yes, there were some detractors who thought the commissioners' indiscretions didn't rise to the level of crimes and certainly not felonies or felonies carrying penalties comparable to second-degree murder. But for the most part, the dispositions in their respective cases were popular. Morrey's hope was that the convictions and sentences would serve as a deterrent not only to those who were inclined to commit embezzlement but any crime of any sort in his district.

When Morrey entered into a plea bargain, something deemed evil by some, many of the protagonists became antagonists. Plea bargaining, if evil, was a *necessary evil*. It merely meant that the prosecution and the defense bargained for a disposition much like tourists might barter or negotiate a price with vendors selling souvenirs. There's no deal unless each side is willing to compromise. The prosecution doesn't want to risk an acquittal, and the defense doesn't want to risk a conviction. Depending on the strength of the case, one side or the other might have to give more than they get. Also, sometimes it isn't so much that a bird in the hand is worth two in the bush but that what is given up is negligible and will have a nominal effect when compared to the benefits.

The editorial in the *Las Cruces Gazette* as well as many of the letters to the editor criticized Morrey for dismissing close to one hundred counts in exchange for a plea to two, as in the case of Madams Grey and Wensel, or dismissing almost as many counts in exchange for two, as in Ben Cromwell's case. Even though Judge Calloway would probably have ordered concurrent sentences anyway instead of stacking them, the antagonists were not appeased.

Morrey felt he was on the horns of a dilemma. If he had spent $100,000 or more on prosecuting all the counts, the same antagonists would have been just as vocal claiming the district attorney's office was foolishly spending the taxpayers' hard-earned money.

No wonder the dispossessed county commissioners had cut the DA's budget. Or, at least, so the detractors would think. To some, prosecuting on all counts would be perceived as overkill and as having no perceptible effect.

He could just see the typical letter-writing condemnation then as well.

Then there were those who thought the sentencing was too lenient and others who thought the sentencing was too harsh. By the former, Morrey was accused of having been bought off and just as bad as the public officials he had just prosecuted. By the latter, he was accused of being vindictive and overzealous.

Even though Morrey was not on the vacancy committee, he was accused of nepotism in the appointment of his investigator's father as a replacement for one of the departing commissioners. The letters to the editor were scathing in that regard, and Morrey's secretary had been fielding some very abusive and threatening telephone calls.

Morrey didn't make prosecutorial decisions based on public opinion. But if he wanted to be reelected to a third term, he had been warned that he'd better take heed. With an election year quickly approaching, Morrey was becoming gun-shy. At least subconsciously, Morrey was giving weight to the political considerations. Even though he didn't want to admit it, he was being swayed somewhat by the winds of public opinion. He had concluded that his next election would not be as much a popularity contest as an opportunity for his detractors to voice their disapproval.

Although Shay Bisben was thought to be an adversary and might be seeking ascension to his throne, Morrey now considered Shay an ally, especially in light of their collaborative effort on the case of the errant commissioners. Shay's attorney's fees on the settlement with the county on the Megan Frye wrongful termination case reputedly netted him over $33,000, which Morrey knew would keep Shay interested in private practice for a long time to come. After all, that was over half of Morrey's annual salary!

• • •

Morrey had heard some rumblings from his father-in-law that Reynard Reid, who had relocated from Denver and was a former assistant attorney general, was interested in Morrey's position. "Rey," as he was called, was in his mid-fifties and a former football star at USC. He was not only physically imposing, but mentally as well. Even though he was a transplant, he had been building quite a following since his arrival. In fact, he was the attorney who successfully represented the daughter killer in the case where a health formula was substituted for insulin resulting in a thirteen-year-olds' death. In some quarters he was considered a savior—saving the innocent from overzealous prosecution. Word was spreading as to his prowess as a trial attorney. He would be a formidable opponent, and Morrey would need to start looking over his shoulder.

• • •

Spring had arrived with a flurry. Mother Nature apparently hadn't received the memo. It was not long, however, before the March weather subsided and the April showers ultimately brought May flowers. Summer meant another major trial with Morrey's nemesis, Reynard Reid.

Bruce Spangberg, the nineteen-year-old son of Dr. Sydney Spangberg, a prominent dentist in Las Cruces, was home on spring break and attending a party at a former classmate's rental house. When one of the female guests, Sandra Torrelli, had left the room to go into the bathroom, Bruce had removed a hunting rifle that had been perched on the antlers of a mounted elk head, and thinking he was clever, loaded it and fired it through the closed bathroom door. The randomly placed slug pierced Sandra's heart and she died instantly.

Vincenti Torrelli, upon learning of his daughter's death and the identity of the killer, went hunting for Bruce with his loaded 30.06. Fortunately, Dr. Spangberg was able to hide his son out at a relative's condo until Vincenti was disarmed and things had quieted down.

After the investigation was completed and it was determined that Bruce, at the time of the shooting, had been smoking marijuana and drinking tequila sunrises and hadn't intended to kill Sandra, Morrey charged him with the crime of manslaughter, a medium-range felony. He didn't charge either first degree murder or second degree murder because he didn't think the act warranted either. Furthermore, intoxication was considered a defense to first degree murder. Manslaughter fit the situation where a person recklessly caused the death of another. It was still a felony, and carried with it a possible prison sentence.

• • •

Vincenti was livid when he learned that his daughter's killer was not charged with murder. His behavior was erratic when he became emotionally distressed, and when he announced to his wife that if the authorities weren't going to seek justice he would, she became concerned.

"What do you accomplish by taking the law in your own hands?" Flo had asked wringing her hands as she paced the floor.

"When the authorities don't do their job, someone has to," Vincenti snorted with disgust. "Do you want our daughter's killer to get off scot-free? When I finish with the bastard, he will be begging to die. What kind of father would I be to just sit nonchalantly by and allow my daughter to be systematically eliminated from the face of the earth?" With that, Vincenti gritted his teeth, and resembling an enraged gorilla, banged his fist thrice against his chest, vowing to seek vengeance.

Flo placed restraining hands against her husband's chest to quell his rage. After regaining his composure, he said with surprising calmness, "Dr. Spangberg's son will never know what hit him. I will seek justice in my own way and in my own time. In the interim, I will confront our inept DA, who obviously is on the take and in my book is as wicked as our daughter's killer. Maybe I can talk some sense into that man!"

• • •

Unannounced, Vincenti strong-armed his way into Morrey's office. Upon hearing the commotion, Toby was immediately on the scene and muscled Vincenti into a half-nelson thus restraining him. Vincenti was not a tall man but was built like a bull. His eyes were glazed and blazing, and with his fists poised for battle, he was obviously prepared to protest Morrey's prosecutorial decision. And it was apparent that his method of persuasion was not going to be by reason or logic. Taken by surprise at the sudden intrusion, Morrey jumped up and rounded his desk.

Although physically restrained, Vincenti was not in the least intimidated. "You're a damn poor excuse for a DA, Dexter," Vincenti snarled. He then jerked his arm from Toby's grasp and demanded, "Take your damn hands off of me." Looking back at Morrey, he shouted, "And to think I voted for you. It's unfathomable that you would validate the murder of an innocent girl by filing, of all things, a manslaughter charge. What's gotten into your head, man? How much did the Spangbergs pay you to look the other way?"

"Just calm down, and I'll give you an explanation," Morrey said as he beckoned Vincenti to be seated.

"Calm down, hell! I don't have time to listen to your evasive commentary and rhetorical gibberish. So, you need not waste your pointless chatter on me." With that, Vincenti started toward the door. Stopping abruptly, he turned, and in a raspy voice, said, "I'll have your political ass on a platter, Dexter, before this is all over—if not before the election, at least at the polls. This time you dug your own grave and deserve to burn in hell."

Vincenti spun on his heels and headed for the open door. Muttering to no one in particular, he sputtered, "I have friends in high places." And turning to Toby, who was still standing in the doorway, he blustered, "Get the hell outta my way! Your boss will soon be ancient history. If I were you, I'd be looking for another job."

• • •

Vincenti had barely left the office when Jenny buzzed Morrey on the intercom, announcing that Dr. Spangberg was on the telephone and wanted to see Morrey *pronto.*

Within the hour, Dr. Spangberg and an attorney Morrey hadn't heard of, a Greeley attorney by the name of Irving Cebes, arrived.

Cebes was the first to speak. "I have been hired by Dr. Spangberg to represent his son on the manslaughter charge," he began. "Not having been a prosecuting attorney, I'm at a loss to understand how it is that a college sophomore with superior educational credentials and an impeccable record is charged with a crime, let alone a felony, in a death involving an accidental shooting."

Dr. Spangberg became emboldened, and not giving Morrey a chance to respond, blurted, "I know it's an election year, and you're trying to make up for the lenient treatment of the county commissioners, but why does my son have to be your sacrificial lamb?"

Morrey, still rattled by Vincenti's intrusion,

realized the volatility of the moment and without taking the time to respond, instructed Jenny to summon Toby. Morrey had wanted him there more as a witness than a bodyguard. Toby, still on an adrenalin high after the Vincenti debacle, immediately stepped inside Morrey's office and closed the door. His fists were clinched at his side and there was blood in his eye—it was apparent he was battle-ready.

Morrey, recognizing Toby was ready to take 'em on, before a brawl could begin, said, "Toby, I wanted you in here to help explain the reason behind our decision to charge Dr. Spangberg's son, Bruce, with manslaughter in the shooting death of seventeen-year-old Sandra Torrelli," Morrey said in an attempt to calm the situation.

"Both Dr. Spangberg and his son's attorney, Mr. Cebes," Morrey began, "have characterized the cause of Sandra's death as *accidental*. They apparently feel that because Bruce didn't intend to kill her, it was an *excusable* homicide, and therefore charges are not warranted."

"Are you contending," Toby, apparently still riled, asked while glaring at both objectors, "that Bruce didn't intend to fire the gun at the door of the bathroom but that the gun just *accidentally* discharged?"

Cebes would field the question. "Bruce said he was just having fun and only intended to scare Sandra. He never at any time intended to cause her death. In fact, he said, if you will excuse the pun, had been hitting on her, as she was a very attractive chick."

"So you admit that the firing of the gun at the door to the bathroom was a deliberate act on Bruce's part, am I correct?" Toby sneered.

"Bruce is not denying that," Dr. Spangberg replied in apparent disgust ignoring Toby's contemptuous tone. "Mr. Cebes tells me that a crime requires not only an act but some kind of corresponding mental state as well. Admittedly, my son committed a regrettable act, but he didn't have criminal intent."

Morrey was back in the fray. He had already turned to two Colorado statutes and placed markers at the proper pages. He first turned to the statute entitled *manslaughter* and read, "A person commits the crime of manslaughter... if such person recklessly causes the death of another person ..." He then turned to the definitions statute and read, "A person acts *recklessly* when he consciously disregards a substantial and unjustifiable risk that a result will occur or that a circumstance exists."

Toby then asked the two objectors, "Do you

think Bruce may have consciously disregarded a substantial and unjustifiable risk that someone could be injured or killed when he knew Sandra was in the bathroom and still loaded and deliberately fired a .30-30 into the closed door?"

"But the door obstructed his view," Dr. Spangberg protested.

"All the more reason he shouldn't have fired knowing that Sandra *might* be in the path," Toby fired back. "What if the roles had been reversed and Sandra had fired into the bathroom door, and it was your son who was killed? Would that have been all right?"

Neither objector responded.

Morrey, fighting hard to restrain his mounting anger, blurted, "You should have been here earlier when Sandra's father was here and irate over me for not having filed murder charges!" Slamming the statute book closed, and glaring at Dr. Spangberg, said emphatically, "I'll bet Vincenti loved his daughter just as much as you love Bruce. The only difference is that you can hug your son today and tell him how much you love him. Vincenti, on the other hand, will not be able to hug his daughter and tell her face-to-face that he loves her—thanks to your son. For you to come in here and tell me your son should not be responsible for killing another man's daughter offends me!

When Dr. Spangberg started to speak, Morrey interrupted. "You can voice your indignation at the polls, as you stated, but how does Vincenti avenge the death of his daughter? Should it be an eye for an eye or a tooth for a tooth? In other words, should he be able to exchange the life of his daughter for the life of your son? Is that what you want? If your son is convicted and goes to prison, he will be released in a few years and be back with you and the rest of your family. Where's the pot of gold at the end of Sandra's rainbow?"

Neither of the objectors said anything further, but Morrey knew that the Dr. Spangbergs of his district and their families and friends would not be campaigning for his reelection. Right now, his focus was not on his reelection, but on seeing that justice was done.

After the objectors left, it took Morrey several minutes to regain his composure. "Dammit, Toby," Morrey said shaking his head. "It all depends on whose ox is being gored. Guess we can't please all the people all the time."

"Hell, we can't even please some of the people some of the time!" snorted Toby.

The two then compared the previous daughter-killer case with the current daughter-killer case. The previous one involved the defendant's daughter; this one involved the victim who was a daughter. In fact, both victims were daughters. Both cases were high profile. Both cases had their protagonists and antagonists. Both cases would divide the community. Both cases would be a no-win as far as the district attorney's office would be concerned. Both would involve jury trials. They hoped the similarities stopped there, especially their respective outcomes.

"I'm damned if I do, and damned if I don't," Morrey lamented. "If we get a conviction in the Spangberg case, we'll make enemies of the Spangbergs and their immense following. If we don't, then we'll make enemies of the Torrellis and their immense following."

"It's already too late with the Torrellis," Toby responded. "They're going to be upset whether there's a conviction or not. Even with a conviction, they won't be satisfied because they perceive you charged too low. And even if you had charged murder one and Bruce got a life sentence, it would be your fault because he didn't get the death penalty."

"And if there is an acquittal, the Torrellis will still want my head on a platter for failure to obtain a conviction of any kind. The Spangbergs will still want my head on a platter for having brought charges in the first place, causing the family expense and grief and causing Bruce to miss the honor roll for the first time in his college career."

"It's a time like this when you need two heads," Toby quipped. "If you're going to be a monster, you might just as well be a two-headed one. That way, both the Spangbergs and the Torrellis will each have a head."

"Very funny! You're beginning to sound like an out of work comedian," Morrey said and swallowed hard.

• • •

Apparently, Irving Cebes thought the better of it and never entered an appearance in the case of *People v. Bruce Spangberg*. Reynard Reid, however, appeared more than eager to defend another daughter-killer and entered his appearance in behalf of Bruce.

A plea bargain was not possible in a case such as this. With the Spangbergs, it was all or nothing. According to them, it was an accidental death and unfortunate, but accidents happen all the time, and the incident would be perceived by the jury as such. Their son was not a criminal and pigs would fly before he would be convicted.

With the Torrellis, on the other hand, Morrey's failure to file murder charges was a mortal sin, an unforgivable one at that, and any further concessions would be the *coup de grace*. Morrey learned that the hard way in the perceived concessions granted to the errant county commissioners. Both sides were backed into the corner, and there was no fudge factor either way.

"There is only one way out of this," Toby said.

"What's that?" Morrey quizzed.

"Present Bruce with the medal of honor. That will appease the Spangbergs."

"What about the Torrellis?"

"I'll see if I can find a hari-kari kit custom-made just for you."

• • •

Despite the Torrellis's vicious campaign, public sentiment seemed to be with the Spangbergs. Vincenti had been somewhat of a rogue in his early youth and owned both liquor stores, one on each end of town. Besides, what was his seventeen-year-old daughter doing at what the newspaper labeled a ruckus college party in the first place? Hadn't she assumed the risk? Why weren't the parents keeping track of their daughter? Who really was at fault in all of this?

• • •

Picking an impartial jury was made all the more problematic because Bruce's father was a prominent dentist in Las Cruces. The jurors, it was thought, might be somewhat reluctant to return a guilty verdict against the dentist's son one day and the next day put their fate in their dentist's hands. *Voir dire* or jury selection was the means by which biased jurors theoretically would be identified and eliminated from the jury panel. Just because jurors promised they would be fair and impartial, didn't necessarily mean that they would.

When a jury with a lot of newbies might be advantageous to the prosecution in light of the dentist connection, through the bad luck of the draw, few reached the jury box, and only one was ultimately selected. Morrey had used up all of his peremptory challenges, and the last juror called was a newbie in her early twenties. She seemed to be intrigued by the defendant who now had shed his facial hair, cropped the thick mat of unruly hair, and sported a dark, two-piece, custom-fit suit, white monogrammed shirt, and ultra-conservative tie—none of which he would have been caught dead wearing not too many months before. No more ponytail, white socks and red tennis shoes reminiscent of his senior prom. He was the all-American college sophomore of which any parent would be most proud.

This was not a field on which Morrey was used

to playing. For the first time since becoming the district attorney, he did not feel as though he had the home court advantage.

The trial judge was the Honorable Roy C. Banyon, a Las Cruces native and a former prosecuting attorney. He was pro-prosecution, at least so Morrey thought, and had been an important ally through many a courtroom battle. Dr. Spangberg, unfortunately, was Judge Banyon's dentist, and Morrey wasn't sure how that would affect the judge's rulings, and it worried him. If Dr. Spangberg was the defendant, it would be an obvious conflict of interest and grounds to disqualify the judge. Here, there were no legal grounds *per se* to disqualify—only supposition. Morrey felt that if Judge Banyon perceived a conflict, he would be disqualifying himself or forced to do so by the chief judge.

• • •

It was a perfect June day with not a cloud in the vast Colorado sky. Two days after Father's Day and the second day of summer, it marked the second day of the jury trial in *People v. Bruce Spangberg.*

After the prosecution and defense made their opening statements, Morrey presented the prosecution's case-in-chief. He called the two investigating officers who collected evidence from the scene, and they identified the crime scene photographs. The weapon, a Marlin Model 1936 .30-30, was introduced into evidence, and through a ballistic expert, it was established that it was the weapon that caused Sandra's death. The county coroner testified that he pronounced Sandra dead at the scene and was the one who retrieved from Sandra's body the slug that was identified by the ballistic expert as the one fired from the .30-30 found at the scene.

A forensic pathologist attributed the cause of death as an implosion of the heart by a projectile that pierced the heart severing the pulmonary artery. He traced the path of the projectile from the entrance wound to the exit wound. He testified that the entrance and exit wounds, and path and damage to the heart were consistent with penetration from an object the size and configuration of the recovered slug. He further testified that his measurements from the bottom of Sandra's feet to the entrance wound were consistent with the location of the hole in the bathroom door. In other words, the projectile that penetrated the bathroom door was the same one that entered Sandra's body passing through her heart and causing her death.

On the third day of trial, seven of the party-goers testified that they witnessed Bruce fire the

.30-30 into the bathroom door. All testified that Sandra was alive when she entered the bathroom and closed the door, and after the shot was fired and upon opening the unlocked bathroom door, all observed her lifeless body. The two detectives who took Bruce's statements testified to having advised him of his constitutional rights and his admitting to having deliberately fired the shot into the bathroom door.

Reid succeeded on cross-examination of the detectives in eliciting Bruce's exculpatory statement that he hadn't intended to hit Sandra but only scare her.

Morrey then announced to Judge Banyon that the prosecution rested its case-in-chief. Reid stated he had a motion to make out of the presence of the jury. Since it was late afternoon, the jury was excused for the day.

Reid made the obligatory motion for judgment of acquittal, which in essence asked the presiding judge to remove the case from consideration of the jury and dismiss the charge because of the insufficiency of the evidence. Such a motion was always made by the defense but seldom granted.

Reid began, "May it please the court. The defense requests dismissal on the grounds that the relevant admissible evidence presented in this case is insufficient to support a conclusion by a reasonably minded jury that the defendant herein is guilty of the charge of manslaughter. Specifically, because the door to the bathroom was closed, not one of the witnesses called by the prosecution testified that they saw the bullet leave the gun and enter the body. The law does not permit conviction based on speculation. Therefore, a dismissal is in order. Thank you, Your Honor."

Morrey, almost fell out of his chair when he heard Reid's reasoning for asking for a dismissal and thus taking the case out of the hands of the jury. In commenting upon the absurdity of the motion and the strong direct and circumstantial evidence presented, opposed the motion. Morrey and Toby were still chuckling to themselves when Morrey returned to the prosecution's table. The motion for judgment of acquittal at the end of the prosecution's case was a pro forma motion, one made as a mere formality. No worry here.

Judge Banyon, without hesitation, made the following ruling: "This court sat through the prosecution's case-in-chief and heard the evidence. At this point, I'm called upon to weigh the evidence and make a determination as to whether or not there is sufficient evidence to sustain a conviction. Unfortunately, from your perspective, Mr. Dexter, I must agree with Mr. Reid that the evidence produced by the prosecution is not of the quantity or quality so as to allow the case to be considered by the jury. As pointed out by Mr. Reid, not one witness herein testified he or she saw the bullet leave the gun and enter the body. For that reason, the court is granting the defendant's motion for judgment of acquittal. The charge against the defendant, therefore, is hereby dismissed, and defendant's bond is hereby exonerated." With that, Judge Banyon banged his gavel and declared the court adjourned. He then headed for his chambers, closing and locking the door behind him.

Morrey was too stunned to do or say anything. He did manage to shake Reid's hand but for the next hour or so was in deep shock. It was all he could do to make it back to his office. Thanks to Toby, he was able to find his way, and in utter resignation, collapsed on the old leather couch in the quiet of his private office.

It would be days before Morrey could even think, let alone function. The two daughter-killer cases had proved debilitating. The first was devastating enough, but this one! This was, without question, the mother of all defeats. He didn't even want to think of all the long-term effects. His sanity was being severely tested. He now needed to rely on a power greater than himself.

Morrey had been exposed to few disappointments, and therefore, had not built up much of an immunity. It was a learning process, and through the love and patience of his family, friends, and Father Edmundo Marquez, the local priest, he was able to ultimately climb out of the depths of despair. A passage of Scripture he would repeat over and over again was: "If you have faith and do not doubt … you will receive whatever you ask for in prayer." He knew his faith would inevitably set him free. But for now, he was literally held captive by Judge Banyon's ruling.

LICENSE TO CONVICT — CARROLL MULTZ

CHAPTER 8

Grace Under Fire

There was no moratorium on criminal activity in Morrey's judicial district, and although the summer may very well be the vacation time for students and educators, it wasn't for those in the criminal justice system. Morrey was able to add a deputy, thanks to the revised budget granted by the new board of county commissioners. That brought his compliment of prosecutors to ten, counting Morrey's assistant and himself. Morrey still had little free time for his family and himself and was more unsure than ever if he wanted the pressures of another four years.

Morrey was able to spend several three-day weekends with Monique, Julia, and Theresa with the Santana clan at the Santana summer home near Rocky Mountain National Park. Even though he was removed geographically, he was still never far from the district attorney's pressures and the constant revisit of and reflection on the two daughter-killer cases that had turned his office and his life upside down. He was plagued by the agony of the two prosecutions and defeats and the repercussions of the county commissioner debacle. He was troubled by his indecision with respect to seeking a third term, and the conundrum in which he found himself was playing havoc with his mind.

Morrey needed distance and space. He was permeated with all kinds of guilt dealing with his personal life. He was becoming withdrawn and spending little time with Monique. Seldom were they alone together, and he didn't want them to grow apart. Monique meant everything to him. Through thick and thin, she was always there administering her undiminished and unconditional devotion and love. She was his strength. It was this realization that caused Morrey to whisk Monique off to Estes Park and the Stanley Hotel, leaving their daughters in the care of their grandparents.

The Stanley Hotel held its own mystique. Known for its ghostly spirits and thought to be the inspiration for Stephen King's *The Shining*, it was built by the cofounder of the Stanley Steamer, F. O. Stanley, in the early 1900s. Those with an interest in the paranormal always stayed on the fourth floor, and if it wasn't already booked, room 418 in particular. F. O. Stanley and his wife, Flora, though deceased for over a half-century, reputedly visit their old haunt and the hotel guests on a regular basis. Even though Morrey and Monique were fortunate to have been assigned room 418, the only strange things to have happened to them there were of their own doing.

While driving back from Estes Park to pick up the girls, Monique and Morrey discussed the pros and cons of Morrey seeking reelection. Both agreed it was a difficult decision but one that needed to be made fairly soon. When Monique scooted closer and kissed Morrey on the cheek, he smiled and said, "The past is history, the future a mystery. Let tomorrow bring what it will. All I want right now is to keep you close and never let you go."

• • •

November 3, the second Tuesday in November, was Election Day, and this year Morrey found he had opposition for the first time in his career. It wasn't Shay Bisben who was opposing him as first thought, but Reynard Reid, the attorney who had opposed him in both daughter-killer cases and who had been triumphant both times.

Three months was not a long time to campaign, and Morrey understood only too well Reid's strategy in waiting to the last minute to announce. It was akin to the sneak attack on Pearl Harbor. Thinking he wouldn't have opposition and waiting to the last minute to announce his bid for a third term, Morrey was unprepared to raise the campaign funds necessary to wage a contested race and organize the campaign committee needed to ensure victory in November. Reid could campaign full-time while campaigning for Morrey would be confined to his off-hours. Being a full-time district attorney prevented him from campaigning during business hours.

Since Reid was a Republican and a member of the other party, Morrey had history on his side. Never in its existence had Paraiso County elected an office holder who was not a Democrat. In fact, in checking the county records, no Republican had outscored a Democrat candidate even in statewide races.

It was obvious Reid was well-funded and well-organized. He had an impressive campaign committee in place. Dr. Spangberg had changed his party affiliation and was Reid's campaign chairman, or more officially, chairman of the Reid for District Attorney Committee; Tracy Cromwell was treasurer. Morrey was not surprised Ben Cromwell's oldest son would spearhead a fundraising campaign against him.

Ever since the acquittal of Bruce Spangberg, the editorials in the *Las Cruces Gazette* had been scathing. It even called into question the disposition of the case of the errant county commissioners. So, it was not surprising that the *Gazette* through its editor, Boyle Lundi, would endorse Reid.

There had been a war being waged against Morrey for the better part of the summer coming primarily from the Torrelli and Spangberg camps. Morrey caught it from both sides of the commissioner prosecution as well. The disgruntled from other criminal prosecutions voicing their dissatisfaction also entered the fray.

There were few pro-Morrey letters printed. If Morrey was to prevail, his supporters would need to mount a counterattack and fill the letters-to-the-editor page with positive reinforcement. He had let some valuable months slip by without having done so. Hopefully, it wasn't too late.

Morrey had told Toby that people either loved or hated him. He had said, "Some people hate to love me, and others love to hate me. Regardless, I still have to be me."

Morrey was looking forward to the inevitable debates he would be having with Reid. He needed to make sure, however, that there were in attendance as many protagonists as antagonists.

He knew having the facts and statistics on his side and the experience factor tilted in his favor would not be enough to combat and overcome the massive and widespread misconceptions created by the local press and malicious gossip. The public scorn for and ridicule of the district attorney's office, and him in particular, was contagious and was now at epidemic proportions.

The first debate was held at the city auditorium in mid-September and was sponsored by the Informed Citizen Coalition (ICC). The challenger went first. He, of course, played the too much plea bargain card and criticized Morrey's office for prosecuting cases he shouldn't and plea bargaining the cases he should zealously prosecute. "It's the district attorney's job to prosecute criminals to the fullest extent of the law and not deal cases in wholesale fashion like it was a fire sale," Reid told the crowd. In an offending tone, he continued, "I pledge that I will not abuse my prosecutorial discretion like Mr. Dexter and not be motivated by my own personal agenda or that of special interest groups."

It was obvious Morrey was offended by Reid's insinuations that he, Morrey, had a personal agenda and played to special interest groups. When he was finally given the opportunity to speak, he started out by asking how many knew what a plea bargain was and its purpose. It was obvious people were ill-advised as to its meaning and were under the impression it was like buying banned goods in the black market. To them it was a deal made in the back room behind closed doors. Whether it was illegal or just unethical, they didn't know. As he sat there listening, Morrey was appalled that most people weren't aware of the reasons and benefits of plea bargaining. He realized it was time to dispel the bogus theories and educate the electorate so he embarked on Plea Bargain 101.

"You may think the way it was postured by Mr. Reid that plea bargaining is evil. It's not. It's authorized and provided for by the laws of this state. Even if you think it's evil, it's a *necessary* evil. We plea bargain over ninety percent of our cases. The DA's annual budget is one point five million. That's to prosecute less than ten percent of our cases. If Mr. Reid prosecutes one hundred percent of the cases, as he just promised, add another thirteen point five million to the DA's budget. Under Mr. Reid's regime, his budget would be fifteen million." Morrey could tell from the reaction of the crowd that his statements were having their intended effect.

Continuing, Morrey stated, "That's twenty percent of our total current county budget. And don't forget the impact his proposed plan would have on the court system and the other agencies that comprise our criminal justice system. If we multiply the five district court judges by eight or nine, we will need at least another forty new district court judges. Instead of five district courtrooms, we will need a total of forty. Are you prepared to pay the taxes necessary to build a new courthouse or hall of justice eight or nine times the size it is now?

"Before you answer that, let me first give you an example of a plea bargain. Because Colorado law requires that all offenses known to the district attorney that arise in his judicial district from the same criminal episode have to be joined in the same charge form or forever be barred, the district attorney is forced to charge every conceivable offense. In other words, he can always drop charges, but he can't add them. Plus, because sentencing can be concurrent, that is, run at the same time and not be stacked one on top of the other, it may matter little if a defendant is convicted of one or two rather than six or eight offenses. Sometimes a defendant is charged with a mix of serious and not so serious offenses such as felonies and misdemeanors and maybe even petty offenses. If the defendant pleads guilty to the most serious, what benefit is it to spend the taxpayers' hard-earned dollars to get a misdemeanor conviction when it would matter little if at all?

"Oftentimes, after charges have been fully investigated, it turns out that some of the charges are not meritorious or the prosecuting witness has changed his or her mind and doesn't want to prosecute. Also, key witnesses often disappear or the alleged cocaine, for example, turns out to be milk-sugar. Do you still persist in your original prosecution, or do you make the necessary adjustments?

"Most cases are not open and shut. Seldom do you catch the culprit standing over the bullet-riddled victim still holding the smoking gun or the culprit admitting to the crime. Normally, in a close case, the prosecution does not want to risk an acquittal by going to trial, and the defendant doesn't want to risk a conviction. They might agree on something palatable to both. Maybe it's a plea of guilty to the charge and a concession made regarding sentencing.

If it's a death penalty case and it's unlikely the defendant would receive the death penalty, the prosecution might make a concession agreeing to a life sentence. The defense might not want to risk the death penalty and may jump at the chance.

"It's a matter of common sense, and the presiding judge has to approve of the disposition. There has to be a compelling reason for the district attorney to make concessions on an open and-shut case, particularly if it is egregious. And defendants are not going to plead guilty to a case where they think they'll be acquitted. It is only in questionable situations where a plea bargain is most likely."

It was now time for questions of and answers from the two candidates. The moderator called on Dr. Spangberg. His question was for Morrey, and being the chairman for Reid's campaign committee, it was obvious it had been prearranged.

Dr. Spangberg stood, and squaring his shoulders, said, "As you know, I have lent my support to Reynard Reid. I did it because I was disappointed you prosecuted my son, Bruce, for accidentally causing the death of Sandra Torrelli. With all the serious cases out there, it was an obvious waste of the taxpayers' dollars, not to mention the grief it caused our family for you to prosecute a case involving a teenage prank gone wrong." Glancing around at the other attendees, he concluded, "My son's vindication is proof of the ill-advised filing of criminal charges. How do you justify your action?"

Morrey wasted no time in defending his decision. "To begin with," Morrey fired back, "your son wasn't vindicated."

Morrey's statement caused a stir among the attendees. Spangberg was on his feet again, "I beg your pardon! My son was vindicated..." he snorted.

Frustrated, Morrey replied, "I beg *your*

pardon!" Morrey then hastened to add, "The judge ruled that because no one saw the bullet leave the gun and enter the body, the case should be dismissed. This is despite the evidence that your son admitted to deliberately firing a .30-30 into a bathroom he knew to be occupied by Sandra Torrelli. Any reasonable person would agree that the rationale cited by the judge for dismissing the case was beyond ridiculous."

"Why you…" But before Spangberg could complete his retort at the mention of the name Torrelli, Vincenti was immediately on his feet. Grabbing one of the microphones, he blurted, "Let me answer the *good* doctor's question!"

A hush came over the fifteen hundred good and noble citizens there assembled. Attempting to control his voice and himself and glaring at Dr. Spangberg, Vincenti said, "If I had walked in here today and deliberately fired my high-powered rifle into the crowd as a prank, of course, and shot and killed Burto, the gentleman seated next to you, would it be okay as long as I hadn't intended to kill him? Is that what you're telling this crowd? If it had been your son who had been killed, would you still be criticizing Mr. Dexter? I'm criticizing Mr. Dexter because he didn't file first degree murder charges against your son for killing my daughter.

I'm not lending my support to either candidate and certainly not Mr. Reid.

"It was Mr. Reid who advanced the absurd defense in your son's case. Quite frankly, I would be worried as hell to elect a district attorney who thinks the killing of an innocent girl is noncriminal if it resulted from a prank. And what a dangerous precedent Mr. Reid has set by establishing that if a witness to a murder is unable to see the bullet leave the gun and enter the victim's body, the murderer is set free. I dare say, if Mr. Reid is elected, there will be no more homicide convictions unless science finds a way for a rifle to fire bullets in slow motion so that they become visible to the naked eye.

"Dr. Spangberg, as we sit here today," Vincenti sneered, "your son is back at his fancy college dorm enjoying life as usual. Because of your son's so-called *prank*, my daughter is lying in a cold, lonely coffin buried six feet below ground at Sacred Heart Cemetery. You speak of your grief over the prosecution of your son. What about our family's grief? Instead of supporting Mr. Reid in his bid to replace Mr. Dexter, why don't you spend your energy on rectifying the devastation caused by your son?"

Vincenti, with clinched fists, had to be restrained as he headed in the direction of Dr. Spangberg.

Dr. Spangberg cowered and began to stutter. Before he could respond, Morrey resumed the reins. "Our office didn't file a first degree murder charge because we couldn't prove Dr. Spangberg's son had the *intent* to kill Mr. Torrelli's daughter. Even if we had, Bruce would have successfully asserted intoxication as a defense. The only homicide charge that fit the offense in light of all the circumstances was manslaughter, and that was the charge we ultimately filed."

The next question was also directed at Morrey. "Why didn't the DA's office file an appeal from that ridiculous ruling in the Spangberg case?"

"The district attorney can, of course, appeal such rulings," admitted Morrey. "However, it's futile, not to mention expensive. If a judge makes an erroneous ruling, as the judge did in Bruce's case, the appellate court can only slap the judge's wrists. Under the law, Bruce is deemed to have been placed in jeopardy by the dismissal, and can't be retried. The double jeopardy provision in the Fifth Amendment to the United States Constitution prohibits persons from being tried twice for the same offense."

Morrey's responses were causing a stir and as the crowd grew unruly, the chair banged the gavel to restore order. Still at the Q and A segment of the debate, the questioning of the candidates continued.

Thought not to be a plant, a cattle rancher by the name of Otis Rivera voiced his indignation over a perceived ill-advised plea bargain. With his lower lip puffed with chew, Otis was blunt and scolding. "Last fall we caught a cattle rustler red-handed and against our better judgment turned him over to the sheriff. We won't do that again 'cause the DA's office just plea bargained the case. The folks ain't very happy 'bout that."

Having just crossed swords with Spangberg and Vincenti, Morrey was ready to take on all comers. "I assume that question is directed at me?"

"Damn straight!" Rivera sneered.

"Mr. Rivera, you remember what the rustler was charged with?" Morrey began.

"I do! Cattle rustlin'. In the old days we'd hung 'em," replied Rivera and looked around obviously seeking support.

"Actually," Morrey calmly responded, "Colorado doesn't have a cattle rustling offense *per se*. The defendant in the case you mentioned was charged with trespass and felony theft. Do you remember what he pled to?"

"All I know is that you fellers plea bargained the case."

"Let me help you with your memory," Morrey

pressed, obviously annoyed at having once again to defend his charging decision. "The defendant's name was Stallings, and he pleaded guilty to both trespass and felony theft. We requested a prison sentence, and he got it. As we speak, he's still serving out his sentence in the Colorado State Penitentiary. There was no plea bargain!"

Rivera bristled, "Yeah, sez you! You never took him to trial—in my book, that's plea bargaining."

Gripping the edges of the podium, Morrey leaned forward and shot back, "Do you realize a defendant has a constitutional right to plead guilty to the charge?"

Rivera, obviously embarrassed, flushed and said, "What…ah, well we didn't know that."

"You don't want the county to spend thousands of dollars on a trial when a defendant is willing to plead guilty, now do you, Mr. Rivera? Wouldn't you consider that a waste of taxpayer dollars?"

Looking sheepish, Rivera answered, "Well, no, now that you put it that way…" It was obvious Otis was looking for a place to hide.

Reid was asked few questions, and the few questions he was asked were by his supporters, for which he had canned responses.

As people entered the auditorium, they were required to fill out a preference sheet indicating their choice for district attorney. The choices were Morris Dexter, Reynard Reid, and Undecided. Upon their exit, they were again required to fill out and turn in an identical form. In the following morning's edition of the *Las Cruces Gazette*, the Informed Citizen Coalition had submitted the following tallies: the entrance polls reflected 61% for Reid, 37% for Morrey and 2% Undecided; the exit polls reflected 28% for Reid, 49% for Morrey, and 23% Undecided.

By the following morning, the Committee to Reelect Dexter District Attorney was organized.

Gazette editor Boyle Lundi and several of the reporters had attended the first debate for district attorney and must have seen the light. By Friday the following week, the newspaper reversed its endorsement of Reid. Apparently Reid was not the Messiah after all. The newspaper justified the switch by admitting it had not only jumped the gun but jumped to unwarranted conclusions as well.

By being resolute, steadfast, and trusting in a power greater than all earthly forces, Morrey was steadily winning over the doubting Thomases in the community. To win his bid for reelection, he would still have to capture the votes of the undecided. He also had to consider that only 1500 out of 24,000 registered voters was hardly a consensus or an accurate barometer. However, it did jumpstart his campaign and win back some of his most ardent detractors.

• • •

Morrey and Reid were asked to speak at the September meeting of the Consortium of Women Voters (CWV). Both candidates, along with their campaign chairpersons and treasurers, were invited. Conspicuous by his absence was Dr. Spangberg. Dr. Spangberg obviously had proven to be an embarrassment to Reid at the previous debate, and Morrey wasn't at all surprised by his nonappearance. Tracy Cromwell, Reid's treasurer and son of former county commissioner Ben Cromwell, did accompany Reid and made a deliberate attempt to avoid contact with Morrey and his entourage.

After their spiel, Morrey and Reid were subjected to some very poignant questioning that resembled a police interrogation. It was obvious the women were split on their endorsement of the district attorney candidates. Diplomacy was not a mantle any of them hid behind. One of the women was a neighbor of the Cromwells while Tracy was growing up. In fact, Tracy and her son were best friends. It didn't take Morrey long to find out for whom she was voting and who was the *personam non gratis* at this gathering.

"This question is for Mr. Dexter," Mrs. Rales announced. "Knowing Ben Cromwell and his family, I have been wrestling with the shabby treatment of a dedicated public servant by a system he helped establish. I don't understand how a county commissioner who has snow removed from his driveway by a county snow plow has committed a crime—especially a felony. Where in our laws does it say that's a crime?"

"Mrs. Rales, you don't need to be a public official to commit theft," Morrey responded. "Anytime you take property without permission from someone else and convert it to your own use, you have committed theft. It doesn't have to be cash; it can be any type of property. If it involves public property and the thief is a public servant, such as a county commissioner, it is deemed to be *embezzlement*, a felony under the laws of this state. And to convert public property to any use other than the authorized public use is also embezzlement. Therefore, conscripting county equipment and personnel for private snow removal is an unauthorized use and *is* embezzlement."

"But Ben was a public official and had the power to decide how county equipment and personnel would be utilized."

"Up to a point," Morrey agreed. "However, neither Ben nor the other two commissioners had the power or authority to commit public property to personal use either for themselves or their family or friends. Public Officials, such as the commissioners and yours truly, are in a position of trust and as such are trustees for the citizens they serve. This means no self-dealing and no conflicts of interest. The law doesn't provide any exceptions. The commissioners took the same oath of office as I did, and that was to uphold the law, not violate it."

"But you didn't have to bring charges against Ben. I can see why you did with the other two, but not Ben."

Morrey was beginning to show signs of fatigue. However, he was the consummate public servant so he politely answered all questions asked of him. "To begin with, Mrs. Rales, I didn't bring the charges. The charges were returned by way of an indictment by a grand jury, which consisted of folks just like you. A special prosecutor appointed by the judge conducted the grand jury; not me. By law, I'm required to prosecute indictments. Otherwise, except in very rare circumstances, I would be violating the law myself and would be hiring someone like Mr. Reid to defend me.

"Secondly, under the equal application or equal

protection of the law doctrine found in the United States Constitution, all persons similarly situated must be treated alike. For the same acts, to prosecute the other two commissioners and not Ben would be disparate treatment, or what we call discrimination. I can't play God and be both judge and jury. Again, I would be as bad as those I prosecute."

"Ben didn't have affairs on the computer as did one or both of the other commissioners, did he?"

"Not that I've been advised. As you know, he was not indicted for having done so. However, many of the other charges were deemed to have been committed by all three."

"Shouldn't Ben's many years of service have been taken into account before indicting him?"

"Why don't you ask Mr. Reid whether that would be a factor he would take into consideration in making a charging decision?" Turning to Reid, Morrey asked, "Mr. Reid, you want to answer Mrs. Rales' question?"

"Not really," Reid said playfully, "but I will. Mrs. Rales, a crime is a crime, and who a person is or was or how important he or she may be, is usually immaterial. It might be taken into account in sentencing but not charging. Now ask Mr. Dexter to respond."

Morrey, looking thoughtful, stated, "Mrs.

Rales, you're not going to like my answer. I think being a public official for as long as Ben had been, placed him in a special category. With all of his years of service, education, and training, it's difficult for someone like Ben to claim ignorance. Instead of being a mitigating factor, it might be considered more of an aggravating factor."

Tracy Cromwell sat there expressionless and remarkably calm. He was difficult to read. If he had contempt for Morrey, it didn't show. He obviously knew Morrey had made sentencing concessions because of his father's age and health, but that was something to commend, not condemn.

The following Monday, it was announced that both Dr. Spangberg and Tracy Cromwell had been replaced on Reid's election committee. Speculation had it that Dr. Spangberg was considered baggage and let go and that Tracy had seen the light and resigned. In either case, it appeared that Reid's election bid was sailing in turbulent waters, and even the fanatics were abandoning ship.

• • •

Morrey's telephone number was not listed in the telephone directory. Only a small circle of intimates could reach him at home. When the telephone rang at 1:45 a.m. that first day of autumn, Morrey knew something was amiss. Half asleep and not holding the receiver close to his ear, he wasn't sure he had heard correctly what Sergio had said.

"Reid what, where, and when?" he heard himself ask.

"Reid's wife called the sheriff 's department worried because Reid had not returned from their cabin or called," Sergio responded. "Two of my sheriff 's deputies, Teague Ruppert and Spike Fosley, took a run up Willard Pass and while rounding Widow's Curve spotted swerve marks leading off into the ravine. Using their portable spotlight, they could see Reid's pickup upside down and perched on some large boulders. When they started down the steep embankment, they spotted Reid's body impaled on a tree limb protruding from a downed pine not far from the truck. Apparently, he had not been wearing his seat belt. Near the truck, they found a shattered bottle of Jack Daniels with the whiskey spill still wet and evident to the smell. When they felt for a pulse and heartbeat, there were none, and he was cold to the touch. Apparently, he had been dead for several hours. An ambulance was called, and his body was transferred to the morgue. The county coroner, Dr. Marquis Claver, officially pronounced him dead and will be performing an autopsy midmorning."

Morrey was speechless and concentrated on

wiping fog and moisture from his eyes as he sat on the edge of his bed in disbelief. Reid was not his favorite person and unofficially was number one on his revised hit list. However, not even his worst enemy deserved this. He felt sorrow for Reid's wife, Claire, and their children and new grandchild. Even though his competition had been eliminated, Morrey could find no peace of mind not then, and as it would prove, not for a long time.

• • •

When told about the liquor bottle and that alcohol may have been involved in her husband's death, Claire thought, No way! She claimed her husband hadn't had anything to drink of an alcoholic nature for over thirty years. She was stunned when she read the toxicology report and learned that her husband's blood alcohol level at the time of his death was a 0.15.

• • •

They had fought contentious courtroom battles and were on the opposite ends of many a controversy. They didn't agree on the law, politics, or religion. Yet there was a mutual respect they had for each other. Morrey never felt Reid had opposed him out of spite or ill-kindred feelings. He knew philosophically they disagreed and came from different perspectives, but they were able to disagree without being disagreeable. Reid, after all, was a worthy adversary and honorable opponent. Morrey would miss the competition and the man.

When Claire called and asked if Morrey would give Reid's eulogy, Morrey was taken aback. At first he was shocked, and apparently sensing he was shocked, Claire stated, "As you may or may not know, Rey had a great deal of respect for you and your legal abilities. He agonized over running against you for district attorney and hoped it wouldn't result in the loss of your friendship. After the first debate, he was second-guessing himself and lamented the fact that he had entered the race. When you hadn't announced and on the basis of some of your earlier statements, he honestly believed you would not be seeking reelection."

"Well, I ..." Morrey stammered.

"Our family would be grateful if you would give Rey's eulogy."

"It...would be my honor, Claire," Morrey managed to respond.

After he hung up with Claire, Morrey was experiencing a mix of emotions. He was feeling grief, sadness, nervousness, regret, confusion, and sympathy—all at the same time. He remembered when his father died that he experienced some of the same feelings plus others like pain, self-pity, anger, despair, resentment, depression, condemnation, anxiety, fear, and guilt. He had become withdrawn and vowed never to get too attached to anyone for fear of being hurt again. He had always been careful not to expose his vulnerability. Monique was an exception to his mantra, "Avoid emotional attachment whenever possible."

Certainly his daughters were exceptions as well.

Mourning the death of a loved one was an exhausting process, and Morrey was determined to make his eulogy for Rey one that would be uplifting, encouraging, and nurturing to Rey's family. He would concentrate on the celebration of Rey's life rather than on the lamentation of his death.

• • •

It was a typical autumn day in paradise. Mother Nature was deserving of a commendation medal this day. With the sun rising high in the blue Colorado sky, family and friends filled all the available seating in Faith Community Church. Morrey guessed there were in excess of 300 in number. Judges, court personnel, and the entire Paraiso County Bar was in attendance to pay tribute to their fallen comrade. Morrey was more nervous than usual and prayed in earnest for divine intervention and inspiration. *Dear Lord, please don't let me falter!*

After Rey's brother, Corbet, delivered "A Family's Perspective," and after Reverend Chapman impressively performed his portion of the ritual, it was Morrey's turn to give the eulogy. Morrey was having a time taming his nerves and emotions. In somewhat of a haze, he tentatively began, "When I was a young boy sitting with my mother and sister at my father's funeral, I heard the preacher, quoting from the Bible, say, 'The day of death is better than the day of birth.' That seemed absurd to me at the time, and it's taken most of my life to realize it's true. Clearly, the destiny of every person is death. No one leaves this world alive. We were born so that we might die, and we must die to be reborn into eternal life. We have to go through the first two stages to reach the third.

"Rey, unlike us, has reached the third stage. It's too bad he and the rest of us have to go through the second stage to reach the third. It's too bad we can't just skip the second stage and proceed directly to that third stage. I don't understand death, and I never have and probably never will. What I do understand is that it's a necessary stopping off point in order to be with God forever in our heavenly paradise. Death is never the end; it's only the beginning. Isn't it strange that everyone wants to go to heaven, but no one wants to die to get there?

"Rey was with us in our earthly paradise. He loved Paraiso and often referred to it by its English translation, 'Paradise.' He never wanted to schedule court on Friday afternoons so that he could spend the long weekends with his wife and family, surrounded by the tall Colorado pines at their cabin. He told me on more than one occasion that when he was there, nothing that was going on in the world seemed to matter and that he felt closer to God there than even in church.

"Rey was the quintessential husband, father, grandfather, son, brother, and friend. His wife, Claire, daughters Mandy and Megan, and new granddaughter, Emily, were the sparkle in his eye. And oh yes, let's not forget Mandy's and Megan's husbands, Torre and Trenton." And looking at the two, said, "He loved you two as well."

After a brief pause, he continued, "Rey was also the quintessential trial lawyer. Boy, don't I know! I would have been able to boast of a perfect record as a prosecutor had it not been for Rey. Not only did he do it to me once, he did it to me twice. After the first, I left the courtroom quickly to avoid his conciliatory handshake. After the second, I readily accepted the victor's handshake and only wish I could do it again. Maybe someday.

"Rey was gracious in victory as well as defeat.

He never showed his emotions. He was always even-tempered and dignified in all the dealings I had with him, even when we opposed each other in the recent campaign. He never lost his sense of humor or ever compromised his ideals. His word was his bond, and if he said he would do something or not do something, you could stake your life on it. As the other attorneys here present will attest, when Rey was on the other side, you knew you better be prepared for battle or you would get whopped.

"Rey fought the good fight and ran the good race. I doubt he would have many regrets. I know we are all the richer for having had him in our lives. Rey, if you are listening, you will continue to be an inspiration to us all. Hope to see you someday in the big courtroom in the sky!"

As Morrey returned to his seat immediately behind Claire, she turned around, and reaching for his hand, whispered, "Rey, I assure you was listening. Bless you for your kind remarks."

Funerals were not Morrey's thing, and he was glad it was over. He was surprised he felt such a loss over a man he had at times considered his nemesis. All of the things he said about Rey today were true, and he would no longer think or refer to him by his last name but only in fond memory as "Rey" or as "a ray."

Morrey understood grief but not the grief of a spouse. He understood the grief of loved ones but couldn't imagine what it would be like to lose Monique or what it would be like for her to lose him. He did know that what Claire was experiencing was traumatic and incapacitating, because he could see it written on her face and see it in her eyes. The grieving process would not be easy, and it would not be quick. Now more than ever, she would need to rely on the loving power of God.

Morrey did go to the graveside service and say his last goodbye. He was struck by the finality of the grave and became emotional when Reverend Chapman concluded with the following:

> *Do not stand at my grave and weep*
> *I am not there, I do not sleep,*
> *I am a thousand winds that blow*
> *I am the diamond glints on snow.*
> *I am the sunlight on ripened grain,*
> *I am the gentle autumn rain.*
> *When you waken in the morning hush,*
> *I am the swift uplifting rush*
> *Of quiet birds in circled flight,*
> *I am the soft star that shines at night.*
> *Do not stand at my grave and cry,*
> *I am not there; I did not die.*

Life was elusive and Morrey promised himself he would make every moment count. The past was the past, and his future was now.

CHAPTER 9

Timing is Everthing

Harvey Beckman was one of two Paraiso County judges. He had been on the bench for almost twenty years. Now in his mid-fifties, he seemed to be locked in his position. Having applied for the district judge's slot on several occasions, he had been denied each time. If he were back in school and receiving a grade for his performance, it would be between a D+ and a C-. He was not well-versed in the law, and his sense of justice left a lot to be desired.

For some time now, he had been making off-the-wall rulings. He was notorious for his reversals by the district court. How he kept being retained in office was due to the general public's ignorance and not by those who appeared before him. Recently, his behavior became as suspect as his rulings.

Morrey had two county court deputies, each serving a county court judge. The one serving Judge Beckman was Nancy Backus, a recent law graduate from the University of Montana School of Law. She had been complaining recently of his treatment of female defendants and what she called a flirtatious attitude toward them and her as well.

Morrey had spoken to the chief district court judge about the situation, but according to Nancy, his actions remained much the same. She had noticed that his clerk, Rachel Quintana, spent a lot of time in the judge's chambers chattering, telling and listening to jokes, giggling, and taking coffee and soda breaks with him. Whether they were engaging in improprieties was uncertain, but the appearances certainly created that impression.

The favoritism foisted on female defendants was no more evident than in two recent trials to the court. One was *People v. Tammy Fox*; the other was *People v. Maria Madena*. The *Fox* case involved a buxom nineteen-year-old cosmetologist caught with a small amount of marijuana in her wallet. Apparently, the marijuana spilled out when she was attempting to produce her driver's license on a traffic stop. Her story was that she had left her wallet on a picnic table at the city park while she and her boyfriend walked the dog, and somebody must have put the dope in her wallet. The traffic cop didn't buy the story but Judge Beckman did, and Tammy was found not guilty.

Just as incredulous was the ruling in the *Madena* case. The audacious thirty-five-year-old mother of two was charged with careless driving and driving with an open container of alcohol. It appeared she had been involved in an accident with a moving train. Fortunately, her children were not with her at the time, and she escaped with minor injuries. With regard to the careless driving charge, she said she had looked both ways as a prudent driver was required to do but just didn't see the train. With regard to the second charge, she said she had just purchased the bottle from the liquor store, and the impact from the train ruptured the container. She brought the salesman from the liquor store into court to establish the timeline that was consistent with her story. Judge Beckman found her not guilty on both charges, ruling that he believed her story and that she couldn't be criminally negligent if she looked both ways.

The other county court deputy recounted a case that he had some years before when Judge Beckman dismissed charges in the middle of a jury trial wherein a twenty-three-year-old female bartender was charged with driving under the influence, leaving the scene of an accident, and careless driving. The evidence was that at 2:30 a.m., a passing motorist heard a crash, went to the scene, and saw that a sport-utility vehicle had crashed into an abandoned building, and he observed a slight figure dart around the corner.

The police were called and in checking the

license plate found it was a vehicle registered to the defendant. When they went to her home less than a block away, she answered the door in what the officers described as a state of inebriation. She claimed that she always left the keys in the ignition of her SUV, and someone must have stolen it.

Because the Good Samaritan couldn't identify her or even say whether it was a male or a female for sure and because the defendant answered the door in her bathrobe, obviously not dressed for travel, Judge Beckman directed a verdict in her favor.

Judge Beckman was known for his flair for fashion and was always impeccably dressed and groomed. Though he had never been married, he somehow fancied himself as God's gift to women. At community functions and service club luncheons, he would be seen talking with or seated next to the young, attractive, and preferably single female of the species. Most appeared to be flattered by the judicial attention.

His courtroom was referred to as the "King's Court." He was the lord and ruler of all who appeared before him. Fraught with pomp and pageantry, he conducted court proceedings as no other. Regal in his black robe and black horn-rimmed glasses, and though genuflecting was not required, he relished in the respect demanded of his position. Although he made a salary of a third or half of the average practicing attorney, it was they who called him "Your Honor."

• • •

So on that first Monday in November following Halloween, Morrey was not surprised when Jenny came into his office while he was talking on the telephone and stuck a note in front of him announcing that Rachel Quintana was there to speak with him.

When Rachel was led into Morrey's office, she appeared tentative. "I'm not sure I should be here," she said in an apologetic tone. "What I have to tell you makes me feel disloyal."

Morrey invited her to be seated and asked if she would like something to drink. Declining, she cleared her throat and said, "As you know, I've been Judge Beckman's clerk for a little over two years now. Harv, as I call him, and I, from the very beginning, have been friendly toward one another and have freely shared our personal matters. Right or wrong, we have exchanged off-colored jokes and kid around quite a bit with each other. It's a freedom we both have permitted, and the informality has been conducive to a productive work environment. But don't get the wrong idea. Other than a hug every now and then, the relationship has been nothing but platonic. Neither of us has crossed the line—that is until just recently."

"Why are you telling me this?" Morrey asked.

Rachel shifted in her chair. It was apparent she was out of her comfort zone and she hesitated. Morrey looked at her and raised his brow encouraging her to go on. She finally continued, "Within the last couple of months, Harv has become touchy-feely. Up to now, the contact has been minimal, and I surmise has been elevated somewhat by Harv's brotherly concern in light of my mother's recent death. I have not discouraged it and in fact have reciprocated at various times when Harv himself appeared troubled."

"But—"

"Please let me finish before I change my mind. Last Saturday, as you know, was Halloween. Around dinnertime I heard a knock at the door. Thinking it was trick-or-treaters, I opened the door with a bowl of candy. Harv had come trick-or-treating in a rabbit costume. And he brought with him an expensive looking bottle of champagne."

Stopping for the moment, Rachel looked reflectively at Morrey and said, "Before I continue, I need your utmost promise that you will keep everything I say confidential. Do I have your word?"

"Of course," Morrey said. "A lot of things are

told to me in strict confidence."

Rachael nodded, and folding her hands together, said, "Anyway, after sharing a couple of glasses of bubbly, Harv became very frisky. I tried politely to discourage him, but he persisted. To keep the situation from escalating, I had to literally push him out the door."

Rachel was now at the point of tears, and after unsuccessfully searching her purse for a tissue, Morrey handed her a box of Kleenex. As she dabbed at her eyes, she continued, "I love my job and actually relish working with and for Harv. As far as a romantic involvement with him, I'm definitely not interested. I have a serious relationship with an ex-classmate, and even if I didn't, Harv is not someone I would be especially attracted to."

"Are you afraid of a reoccurrence?"

"Yes," Rachel immediately responded. "Actually, I'm afraid Harv's aggression will escalate and spill over into the workplace. I've never intentionally led him on and wonder if the bubbly might have interfered with his usually good judgment, and that the whole affair was just an aberration."

When Morrey asked what he could do, Rachel said she just wanted someone she could trust to know about the situation. Harv was attending a meeting at the probation department, and this was the ideal time to visit without alerting or alarming him or anyone else. She said she better get back to her office and asked if she could return and seek assistance should the circumstances warrant. She again cautioned Morrey not to say anything to anyone. Morrey reassured Rachel that he would keep the matter confidential and would be available should the need arise.

After Rachael left, Morrey reflected on the situation, and reconsidered his pledge of confidentiality, feeling that perhaps Toby should be brought into the loop. He did it for two reasons. One was to get Toby involved at an early stage and be available in case he was needed. The other was to be Morrey's sounding board.

Morrey's concern about Rachel's safety was also shared by Toby. They were really on the horns of a dilemma. If they intervened prematurely, they would probably end up with egg on their face. If they waited too long, they might lose their advantage and allow Judge Beckman to not only cover his tracks but strike again.

• • •

For a long time now, Morrey felt that somebody up there must be looking out for him. Before he had time to agonize over a decision, Sergio was already on the telephone the following morning advising him that the night before, two of his deputies had responded to Rachel's 911 call. Apparently, in asserting himself, Judge Beckman had roughed up Rachel, and she was pressing charges. Judge Beckman spent the night in the county jail and was expected to bond out first thing that morning. The press had already caught wind but too late for the morning edition.

"Can you believe that?" Sergio asked.

"Actually, yes," Morrey responded, and looking heavenward, said, "I can."

• • •

Since it was Election Day, Morrey stopped by his designated polling place and voted for his favorite choices for district attorney, sheriff, and county commissioners. Being unopposed,

Morrey had no worry about the outcome of his race or Sergio's. And if the truth were known, no worry about the commissioners' race either. He would sleep well this night.

On the way out of the polling place, Morrey ran into Toby. Waiting for Toby to cast his ballot and fielding another phone call from Sergio on his cell phone, he advised a stunned Toby of the latest development in the saga of Judge Beckman.

When they arrived at the district attorney's

office, Sergio was already waiting for them. Since Rachel's home was located in the county, the sheriff 's office had jurisdiction. Sergio advised that the two investigative/arresting deputies, Carlos Sartan and Palen Jeffers, were on their way over with the offense report. While they waited for the deputies, Sergio stated that Judge Beckman apparently had tried to kiss Rachel, and when she slapped his face, he slapped hers. When he refused to leave, Rachel called 911.

When Judge Beckman was arrested later at his home, the deputies reported he was in rabbit attire. He had a strong smell of alcohol on his breath, and his only reply when confronted with Rachel's allegations was that "She slapped me first!" Even to the most casual observer, this was hardly a fitting thing to do to a judge, especially Judge Beckman.

After reading the offense report and conferring with the deputies, it was decided that criminal charges were warranted. The unwanted kiss was an assault. Slapping Rachel's face was a battery, and refusing to leave her home upon request was a trespass.

After much discussion, it was decided that the district attorney's office would file the following charges: assault in the third degree (knowingly or recklessly causing bodily injury to another), a misdemeanor; and first degree criminal trespass (knowingly and unlawfully remaining in a dwelling of another), a felony.

Because of the special circumstances of the case, Morrey was allowed to file charges by way of information directly in district court. Until an outside judge could be appointed, Chief District Court Judge Pinkerton T. Calloway would handle the preliminary matters. At the bond hearing and advisement of rights, Judge Beckman, without his black robe or rabbit costume, was somewhat subdued and was later described by the press as the ignominious judge, a label that would follow him into eternity.

Morrey did not oppose a personal recognizance bond, and the judge also known as the rabbit as well as the ignominious judge announced he would represent himself (i.e., appear pro se). It was certain in that packed courtroom that the axiom, "He who represents himself has a fool for a client," crossed everyone's mind. It certainly was a cause to chuckle—especially for the prosecution team.

• • •

Rachel, thinking the better of it, came into Morrey's office the following day wanting to drop charges against Harv. His antisocial behavior she attributed to too much bubbly. Her mantra was no harm, no foul. Morrey was reminded of all the women who appeared on his doorstep on Monday mornings wanting their husbands or significant others released from jail and all of the weekend domestic violence charges dropped. The hooch was the devil that made their man do it—just an aberration or a fluke until the next occurrence.

Upon submission of his immediate resignation from the bench and a guilty plea to the misdemeanor with a guarantee of probation, the pending felony charge would be dropped. In addition, the soon-to-be-defrocked judge would have to submit to mental health counseling. This was a plea agreement to which Rachel would agree and to which Chief Judge Calloway would affix his *imprimatur*.

• • •

Things had been going Morrey's way. He was on a roll. Election Day saw his overwhelming endorsement for district attorney and garnering the largest number of votes for a local candidate next to Sergio. All three of the replacement county commissioners were elected to staggered terms, with Toby's father, Milton, receiving a full four-year term since it was he who replaced Ben. Also, Milton would later be designated chairperson by his fellow commissioners. It wasn't likely either the district attorney's office or the sheriff's department would need to be worrying about their budgets, at least not for a long, long time.

• • •

With the vacancy now on the county court bench, there was a concern over who the governor would appoint as a replacement. The DA's office didn't want anyone as inept as Harv or someone even worse. Shay Bisben was someone who had come into his own and an attorney the community had come to admire and respect. When asked to consider the position, Shay unhesitatingly acquiesced. Although several other attorneys were interested and submitted applications, Shay was the one the governor ultimately selected. Competency, dedication, and lack of arrogance would hold Shay in good stead. Shay was a welcomed change to the bench.

CHAPTER 10

Redemption

It was Thanksgiving break, and college students were returning home for the holiday. Bruce Spangberg was just concluding the first semester of his sophomore year at Colorado State University in Fort Collins. Driving the BMW he received as a birthday and early Christmas gift from his parents and showcasing a fellow classmate and head-turner by the name of Dorinda Sessions from Coeur d'Alene, Idaho, Bruce descended on Las Cruces. Whether the party crowd was ready or not, Bruce was back for action.

Dorinda would be staying at the home of Dr. Spangberg and his wife, Sorena. Dorinda would be occupying Bruce's sister's room, as Julie was away attending school at Creighton. Being a camera buff, Dorinda was anxious to spend time at the Spangberg cabin in the aspens and pines on the western slope of Stead Mountain. Partly to distance themselves from the watchful eyes of Bruce's parents and partly to take advantage of the passing of the season, Bruce and Dorinda left to spend Thanksgiving eve at the Spangberg Stead Mountain retreat.

• • •

When Bruce arrived home Thanksgiving Day, well in advance of the time for the scheduled feast, he was Dorinda-less. Bruce, of course, was questioned by his parents as to Dorinda's absence. Almost rehearsed, he responded, "On her way back here, Dorinda received an SOS on her cell phone from her roommate. Dorinda said she was worried about Alison and needed to return to Fort Collins to console her. Dorinda refused my offer to drive her back to Fort Collins. She was worried about disappointing the two of you. So I dropped her off at the bus station in time to make the one thirty departure."

"What in the world!" Bruce's mother exclaimed with a frown. "I hope in whatever predicament Alison has found herself that Dorinda will be of help. And what is to become of the clothing and personal effects she's left behind in Julie's room?"

"She has with her the items she took to the cabin," Bruce replied. "What she left behind I can return to her when I get back to school. In the interim, I doubt she will miss them."

• • •

Back at school and no Dorinda, and Dorinda's parents having been advised that their daughter had gone home with Bruce, were understandably confrontational. Bruce's explanation to them raised suspicion so much so that the authorities were soon called in. Dorinda's disappearance caught the attention of the print and broadcast media as well. Soon her photograph and story was on the front page of every newspaper in the state, including the *Las Cruces Gazette*. It raised the antenna of the district attorney's office, and it was not long before local law enforcement was involved in a massive manhunt.

Sergio and several deputies, accompanied by Dr. Spangberg, did a cursory search of the Spangberg cabin, grounds and surrounding area. There was no sign of Dorinda or any visible evidence of foul play. Sergio, however, grew suspicious when he checked with the bus company and found there was no record that Dorinda had booked a bus ride.

When Bruce was interviewed by Sergio, Bruce appeared tentative and evasive. "What time did you drop Dorinda off at the bus station?" Sergio inquired.

"Right around one p.m.," Bruce responded. "I remember looking at the clock on the wall when we arrived, hoping the bus had not already left."

"We have interviewed the manager and the ticket counter personnel who were on duty at the time, and no one remembered Dorinda having purchased a ticket or even having been there."

Bruce jammed his hands into his jeans pockets and looked around before answering. "I'm upset with myself for not waiting to make sure she purchased her ticket. We were already late for Thanksgiving dinner at my parents' home, and I didn't want to keep everyone waiting."

"In speaking with your mother, we were told dinner was not scheduled until four p.m. Was she incorrect?"

"Actually, I thought she said dinner would be at one p.m. It was my mistake. I didn't realize that dinner would be at four until after I arrived home."

"Did you check to see if Dorinda had the necessary funds to purchase a ticket? By the way, how much was the ticket?"

"I don't know how much the ticket cost. I didn't check. But I left her fifty dollars, which I thought would be more than enough to get her home."

"The manager told us that a one-way ticket to Fort Collins cost sixty-five dollars," said Sergio, as he flipped through the small notepad he took from his breast pocket.

"She had her purse with her, and I'm sure she had more than enough to cover the difference."

"But you don't know that for sure, do you?"

"No, not really. She was not broke. I do know that."

"By the way, the manager also told us that there was no one thirty p.m. departure time scheduled for Fort Collins. One bus had left at noon, and the next was not scheduled to leave until three p.m."

Bruce began to squirm and answered, "They must have changed schedules unbeknownst to me. The last I knew there was a one thirty p.m. departure to Fort Collins."

"So, let me understand what you've told me so far. Dorinda received a distress call from her roommate, Alison. Alison never told Dorinda what the problem was all about only to get back to Fort Collins ASAP. Correct?"

"Yes."

"Now, this was on a Thursday, Thanksgiving Day, and the two of you were scheduled to return to Fort Collins on Friday, the following day. Correct?"

"Yes."

"Neither Dorinda nor her roommate could wait until Friday?"

Avoiding eye contact with Sergio, Bruce went on to explain, "I questioned her about that and even offered to drive her back Thursday night. She was adamant about me being with my parents and not interrupting my stay. I didn't want to argue with her, so I let her have her way."

"Going back to the time you dropped her off at the bus station, you didn't wait to see if she purchased a ticket and didn't wait to see if she boarded the bus. Is this what you're telling me?"

"Yes, I thought I was already late for dinner."

"That was at one p.m., and yet dinner was not scheduled until four p.m."

"As I told you, I was incorrect about the time. In retrospect I would have waited to make sure Dorinda boarded the bus. I've been kicking myself ever since."

"When you say 'been kicking myself ever since,' what exactly do you mean? Do you think something bad has happened to Dorinda?"

"I can't say. All I know is that I've not heard from her."

Sergio, looking squarely at Bruce, asked, "What do you think might have happened to her?"

"Don't know. If she didn't take the bus as you state, then she probably caught a ride with someone else."

"Do you think she would accept a ride with a stranger?"

Bruce's pattern of lying when confronted was a way of life since childhood. He answered, "Well, she's not from this area, and it's highly unlikely she would run into someone she knew. So, yes, it was probably with a stranger."

"Did you ever call to see if she made it home all right?"

"I was upset with her for leaving and felt the ball was in her court. I wasn't about to initiate the call."

"Is that the reason you didn't try to reach her when you returned to school?"

"I figured she was okay, and I was still upset she had abandoned me and stood up my parents."

Sergio wasn't buying Bruce's story—it had too many holes in it. Sergio pressed on, "Did you attempt to return the clothing and personal effects Dorinda had left at your home?"

"No. I did take them back to school, but I threw them into a dumpster at my apartment complex when I hadn't heard from her. Remember, I was still upset with her."

• • •

Dorinda's disappearance was now receiving nation-wide attention. Between receiving pressure from Dorinda's parents and being hounded by the media literally from around the globe, it was obvious Morrey was behind the eight ball once again.

"Applying the smell test," Toby said, "Bruce's story stinks." Both Morrey and Sergio agreed.

"Bruce has killed one girl and now perhaps another," Morrey speculated.

All knew they had to get to the bottom of the matter and that no one would rest until they did. No one had seen Dorinda after she had left with Bruce to go to the Spangberg cabin. They weren't sure the two ever made it to, or more likely, from the cabin. They were fairly certain she never left Las Cruces—not by train, plane, car, or bus. They knew she never made it back to school or at least not back to her dorm.

When her roommate was interviewed by Fort Collins authorities, she denied having telephoned Dorinda or having summoned her aid. Neither the dorm assistants nor Dorinda's roommate saw Dorinda after she left on Thanksgiving break. Dorinda's instructors confirmed her absences when classes resumed after break. The last telephone call Dorinda's parents received from their daughter was Thanksgiving eve when she excitedly reported that she was in transit with Bruce to the Spangberg cabin on Stead Mountain.

The investigation into Dorinda's disappearance was going nowhere. There was an abundance of circumstantial evidence pointing in Bruce's direction. However, Dr. Spangberg apparently sensing his son was a prime suspect and not wanting his son to be prosecuted for a crime he didn't commit, made Bruce off-limits to the press and to the authorities at both Las Cruces and Fort Collins. Even though Bruce said he would take a polygraph, Dr. Spangberg squelched any attempt to do so.

With the speculation in the press and the authorities breathing heavily down Bruce's neck, Dr. Spangberg hired an attorney from the western part of the state who was known for his magic in materializing acquittals for his clients. Luhan Montez was known as the Merlin or Katerfelto of the courtroom. Caught red-handed, chained in condemnation, and nailed to the cross by their own confessions, Montez's clients somehow managed to escape the clutches of the law. His recrimination tactics usually resulted in his clients' accusers being the ones put on trial.

Montez was all of six feet four inches tall. With broad shoulders, a barrel chest, a bull-like neck, and heavy features, he might have been mistaken for a linebacker for the Chicago Bears. However, with thick, rich hair, tanned skin, deep, dark reflective eyes, pearl-white teeth, an ingratiating smile, and a movie star swagger, he was a cross between Cary Grant and John Wayne. His courtroom theatrics made everyone wonder if maybe there was a Hollywood connection. Quick-witted, intuitive, intelligent, observant, and having a natural legalistic cadence, his adversaries were no match for Montez. He had a pleasant hypnotic voice that could charm even the most ardent detractors. His strategy was to lull his opponents into submission, and if that didn't work, beat them to death. Whatever tactic he employed, his opponents were defeated before they even began.

Montez's retainers were usually in the six-figure bracket, and depending on whether it was a death penalty case, could even be in the sevens. When it came to fees and factoring in the degree of difficulty he followed the mathematical rule of three. He lived and skied in Aspen and not only hobnobbed with the rich and famous but was one of them, and it was usually they who sought him out. So far, no David had succeeded against this Goliath.

The rules of engagement required the client to be totally subservient and follow any edict Montez would issue. If you disobeyed his commands, you would immediately hear the Montez version of the dreaded Trump farewell declaration. Even his most powerful clients trembled at the thought. It was a case of "Montez knows best, and I'd better follow his advice." So far, however, no client had been disappointed.

Montez's first order of business was to advise

the law enforcement community that he was representing Bruce Spangberg and that neither they nor their agents were to have any contact directly with Bruce. His office would be the conduit for any desired communication.

The media also received similar instructions.

With Montez in the mix, the paparazzi were all over the CSU campus, shadowing Bruce's every move. Presumably upon instruction from Montez, Bruce dropped out of school at least for the time being. Bruce then went into hiding and reputedly was sequestered on a remote island in the Pacific, where he would be safe from the prying eyes of the media and curiosity seekers.

• • •

Both Dr. Spangberg and his wife had been trust babies. Dr. Spangberg became a dentist not because he was particularly dedicated to the profession or because of the remuneration aspect, but to attain respectability and prestige. He had the money, and he was willing to spend it all, if necessary, to vindicate the dignity of his much-maligned son and to clear the Spangberg name.

Neither Morrey and the district attorney's office nor Sergio and the sheriff 's department were the least bit intimidated by Montez's involvement in the Spangberg investigation nor were they deterred in their quest to make Bruce pay for his sins. However, without a corpus delicti, there wasn't enough to charge, let alone convict.

The investigation had reached an impasse. Law enforcement at both ends and at all levels was growing increasingly frustrated. Even Morrey was on the brink of despair. It was possible Dorinda was still alive, but it was highly improbable. Morrey and the others were convinced that Dorinda never came down from Stead Mountain. To think it was one thing, but to prove it was something entirely different.

• • •

From the time she was three years old, Crystal Cantrell had visions about occurrences that never made it into the history books and events that were not yet. Her daydreams and wild imagination had resulted in her parents' recrimination, stern scolding, and sometimes harsh consequences. Her seeing and talking to angelic figures, which she referred to by name, seemed harmless at first but resulted in her ultimately being placed in the care of psychologists and psychiatrists.

To avoid the label of a psychotic and all that went with it, Crystal convinced her parents and the experts that she had outgrown her grim and sometimes morbid childhood musings. Her charade, however, was exposed shortly after she entered the second grade and in a dream saw her paternal grandfather crushed after tumbling into a hay bailer on his Iowa farm and going to be with the Lord. Risking the consequences, Crystal reported the event. Crystal being in tears and somewhat hysterical, her parents wrote it off as a nightmare. Nonetheless, they called her father's parents and found Gramps to be alive and well. Three days later, however, they received a frantic call from Crystal's grandmother relaying the distressing news that Gramps had fallen into a hay bailer and been killed.

After extensive testing by a parapsychologist, it was determined that Crystal had not been fabricating, imagining, or hallucinating but had psychic or paranormal powers. She was a *bona fide* psychic, a clairvoyant. No longer would she be accused of being a daydreamer but credited with having extrasensory perception. Instead of being condemned, she was now commended.

She had a special gift from God, and her parents made her promise she would use it wisely.

Morrey had learned of Crystal through a district attorney in the Greeley area who had used the remarkable clairvoyant some years before to locate a missing woman in their jurisdiction who they thought to be the victim of foul play. Never having been to Colorado and not being told much about the circumstances, Crystal led them to the remains and ultimately to the perpetrator. Morrey determined she was the same clairvoyant who helped the parents locate the body of their young son who had drowned in the Colorado River some years later.

What did they have to lose? Toby and Sergio were somewhat skeptical at first, but being anxious to get the case off dead center, they were willing to try anything. They all agreed they would say nothing to anyone, especially if it proved to be futile. They didn't want to appear as fools. Obtaining Crystal's telephone number from Morrey's counterpart in Greeley, the three were poised by the speakerphone to talk to the renowned Crystal Cantrell. They weren't sure they would reach her on the first try, but they did.

"Ms. Cantrell, this is Morrey Dexter in Las Cruces, Colorado. I'm the district attorney for this area and just starting my third term. With me on the speakerphone are my investigator, Toby Kincaid, and our long-time sheriff, Sergio Santana."

Without any greeting, Crystal said, "Sheriff Santana is your father-in-law, is he not?"

The three were speechless. *Wow*, they all

thought. Sergio admitted to being Morrey's father-in-law and then asked, "How'd you know?"

"Just did," she responded. "You want me to locate a missing person, a coed?"

"Why, yes," Morrey replied. When Morrey tried to tell her about the case, she politely interrupted him and advised him that she would be more effective in assisting them with the less she was told.

Because it was winter, she was indisposed until after the first of the year. "Besides," she continued, "it won't do any good to visit the high country until after the snow melts, and that probably won't be until April or May."

Still somewhat in shock as to how much she knew, Morrey replied, "We, indeed, will be taking you into the high country as the starting place of your psychic investigation. Depending on the intensity of the snow melt, the area could be accessible in early or mid-April. I take it you don't want us to send you any reports or other information?"

Respectfully declining the reports, Crystal assured Morrey and the others that they could provide whatever information they wanted and ask whatever questions they had at a later time. She said she had a protocol that she preferred to follow that would be in everyone's best interest.

They were hoping for a quick fix. Solving the mystery now would make them and their constituents all sleep better. They knew the answers to the puzzle were hidden on Stead Mountain and that they couldn't do much digging until the snow disappeared. The investigation would just have to remain in limbo until spring. Crystal had made that crystal clear.

• • •

It was late on that clear, sun-filled Friday afternoon, the last day in April, when Morrey and Toby picked Crystal Cantrell up at the Paraiso County airport. The two were taken aback by Crystal's starlet good looks. She was not at all as they had imagined. Her blondish hair, light complexion, fine features, and sparkling greenish-blue eyes bespoke of her Nordic ancestry. She was so striking that they almost hoped they would be seen with her, as that would certainly enhance their public image. What their wives would think, however, might be a different story.

Morrey and Toby delivered Crystal to the El Hotel Palacio, Las Cruces's finest. Helping with her luggage and waiting until after she had checked in, she was left alone as she had requested.

• • •

Armed early the next morning with a search

warrant and an ice chest full of food and drink for the day, Sergio, along with his passengers, Morrey and Toby, finessed the oversized sheriff 's department van under the portico of the El Hotel Palacio and parked directly in front of the main doors. Dressed in blue jeans and appropriate country attire and blending in with the natives, Crystal was waiting for them. With nothing more than a handbag, she joined the trio.

As they exited town and journeyed along the main road in the direction of Stead Mountain, the small talk stopped. "This is the way the two traveled the afternoon of Thanksgiving eve. The young woman nestled close to the young man as soon as they started the long climb up Stead Mountain, starting right about there," she said as she pointed in the distance. "Both were eager to be alone and happy to be away from the young man's parents. The two, were in their early twenties and had been a thing for almost a year and a half. He's tall but husky with dark hair and dull, dark eyes. He's always joking, and I see him pulling a flask of what smells of whiskey blend from beneath the driver's seat. He takes a drink and hands it to a rather tall, auburn-haired, brown-eyed knockout. I see her taking a rather generous swig."

As the four wound their way up the rugged

mountain, Crystal grew quiet once again, and Sergio could see through the rearview mirror that she was preoccupied and in deep concentration. Her eyes narrowed, and he could see the deep furrows forming between them. Just as they rounded Widow's Curve, she groaned, "You're driving too fast; please slow down!" As if in a trance, she yelled, "Oh my God, look out for that branch! Too late," she sobbed.

Morrey, Toby, and Sergio knew that was the exact spot where Rey took his last curtain call. But how did Crystal know? The three were having a difficult time coming to grips with the fact that Crystal was a psychic. Her distress was fading as they kept driving, and she was regaining her composure.

"All three of you knew the man who ran off the road around that curve, didn't you? There have been others who, over the years, have met their fate there as well. This was the only one, however, who was impaled by a tree limb." Looking into Morrey's eyes, as he sat next to her, she said, "I watched as you said kind things about the man at his funeral. Even though you're a prosecutor, you have a sensitivity and a compassion not common for too many prosecutors. I sensed while you were speaking, however, that you felt some guilt and maybe considered yourself a hypocrite."

Morrey was beginning to feel self-conscious, vulnerable, and exposed. He hoped she hadn't detected that momentary lust he felt when he first focused his eyes on hers at the airport. He would have to be careful what he did, said, and thought. There would be no room for error, not with this one. He only hoped she would understand and would be forgiving. He didn't want to offend her.

As they were nearing the cabin, they came to a fork in the road. "Turn right here," Crystal said. "The left fork," she added, "is the road the young man took in a four-wheeler while towing a trailer."

Crystal, staring at the landscape, said it was the identical landscape she had pictured in her mind while talking with Morrey, Toby, and Sergio on the telephone back in December. Still over two miles from the Spangberg cabin, Crystal described the cabin with architectural precision. She even accurately described an outbuilding that she claimed housed the four-wheeler and trailer the young man drove down the left fork of the road.

Although Sergio had been at the cabin right after Dorinda's disappearance, neither Morrey nor Toby had ever been there. And of course, neither had Crystal. As the cabin came into view, Morrey and Toby were astounded because even to the minutest detail, it was as Crystal had described. After they stopped and exited the van and as Crystal was about to ascend the three steps to the front decking, she stopped abruptly. Going over to the inside edge of the first step, she stooped over, and while brushing some dead grass aside, exposed a ring she said belonged to the young woman—the same young woman who she had envisioned riding next to the young man she had described on the way up the mountain.

With the investigative kit Sergio was carrying, he retrieved the ring and placed it in a plastic bag that he sealed and then deposited in a zippered evidence pocket that was part of his evidence kit. In the same location as where the ring was found, Sergio also collected a belt loop that appeared to have once been attached to a pair of blue jeans. Crystal immediately identified the belt loop as having come from the blue jeans the young woman had been wearing at the time of her death.

The minute Crystal set foot in the unlocked cabin, she entered into what Toby would later describe as a hypnotic state or trance. Whether in a hypnotic state or trance or just a state of deep concentration, Crystal appeared to be in a different dimension. It was confusing to the three observers, because while she was watching events of the past unfolding, she was carrying on a coherent conversation with them in the here and now. Careful not to distract Crystal, the three said nothing and just listened while Toby took copious notes.

The most chilling of the whole psychic investigation was when Crystal became Dorinda and relived the grim events leading to Dorinda's death. In elaborate detail, she suffered the horror and excruciating pain inflicted on the poor, helpless, now-missing young woman. It was an instant replay of the criminal homicide, costarring Bruce Spangberg and Crystal Cantrell as Dorinda's stand-in.

Crystal was the eyewitness of which every prosecutor dreamt. The only problem here was that such testimony was and is inadmissible in a court of law. The testimony of a clairvoyant is not deemed to have scientific validity. It fits in the category of speculation and conjecture, and is therefore, thought to be unreliable. It could lead to the discovery of otherwise admissible evidence, however, and that is wherein the value of a clairvoyant's perspective would be found. So far, the prosecution team had not been disappointed.

Crystal's performance was like filming segments for a movie. There were different takes, and the sequence would await editing. When editing was complete, there would be a coherent progression, and all the pieces would be logically and ultimately sequentially connected. Removed in time and space, Crystal was able to reconstruct the following chain of events:

"The killer was the son of prominent old family residents of Las Cruces. The father had coddled his only son and covered and made excuses for him his whole young life. The son had a split personality and relished playing the part of the bad son. The bad son side was the dominant side and even when he played the part of the good son was still very narcissistic and sadistic. When he didn't get his way as a child, he threw a tantrum, and as an adult, became violent. He had few friends because of his temper. His fraternity brothers referred to him as a party animal, and when he drank, he was unpredictable and uncontrollable. The amount of alcohol did not seem to be a factor; any amount became fire water."

With her eyes still closed, Crystal said, "I can see the young woman, but I can't put a name to her."

"Her name was Dorinda," Morrey replied. "And the young man's name was Bruce Spangberg."

"Dorinda held a secret she had been hiding from Bruce. It wasn't until after they had been intimate at the cabin and both had consumed their fair share of alcohol that Dorinda revealed the secret."

Crystal then paused momentarily as Morrey, Toby, and Sergio waited in eager anticipation.

"Dorinda was three months pregnant!" Crystal said as she opened her eyes. Apparently noticing the astonished expression written across the faces of the three, she related, "Bruce was upset because Dorinda hadn't told him sooner, and he felt deceived. He also felt deceived in believing that she had been on the pill. When the issue of abortion came up and Dorinda said she couldn't for moral and religious reasons, Bruce became enraged."

Crystal hesitated for a moment, and shaking her head, seemed absorbed by an image being formed in her mind. She appeared distressed and after a long pause continued, "Bruce was a master of verbal abuse, and Dorinda had always been submissive and compliant. This time, however, she stubbornly resisted his attempt to dominate her. She made the unpardonable mistake of throwing a glass of cold water in his face. He thereupon used Dorinda as a punching bag. When she broke free and started for the door, he grabbed the closest thing he could find, a poker by the fireplace. To prevent her escape, he hit her over the head with it. The blow crushed her skull instantly causing her death."

Crystal related, without even going to the outbuilding, that "Bruce then dragged Dorinda on the blood-stained carpet through the front door and onto the deck. He then hitched a small trailer to the four-wheeler that he had retrieved from the outbuilding and drove it to the front of the cabin. There he wrapped Dorinda in the carpet and hoisted the rolled corpse into the trailer. He tossed fallen pine boughs on top, disguising its contents. Since it was too late and too dark to dispose of his cargo, he waited until the next morning to do so.

"At daybreak, taking the left fork which would be to his right upon leaving the cabin, he drove the slash-covered body to a dump site ten miles away. Finding the access blocked by a padlocked gate, he went into the woods a mile behind the dump, and using a shovel he had brought with him, buried Dorinda and the blood-stained carpet, poker, towels, and a satchel containing her clothing taken from the cabin in the same shallow grave. The slash was placed on top to camouflage the gravesite. Realizing that he had forgotten to dispose of Dorinda's purse and toiletries when he arrived back at the cabin, Bruce buried them under the dirt floor of the outbuilding." Crystal then frowned and rubbed her temples. "You'll find the purse buried beneath an old, rusted oil drum that has a spare tire and rim sitting on top," Crystal told Sergio.

In the cabin, they checked around the fireplace to see if indeed the poker was missing. It was. They next observed in front of the fireplace a rectangular configuration where the wood was darker than the rest of the floor. It measured five-and-a-half feet by seven-and-a-half feet. In checking the bathroom, they found an empty towel rack by the bathtub/ shower. Sergio seized hand towels and washcloths from a cabinet, which he assumed would match the towels he hoped would be discovered with the carpet, poker, and Dorinda's body. Photographs were taken of all areas of the cabin.

When they went to the outbuilding, they discovered the four-wheeler and trailer just as Crystal had described. And not surprisingly, they spotted the old, rusted oil drum with the tire and rim on top. Careful not to obliterate any fingerprints, they moved the tire and rim to one side, then the drum. They observed that the ground was soft and appeared to have recently been spaded in the area where the drum had sat. While all of this was being performed, Toby had his video camera rolling. Instead of using the shovel leaning against the wall near where the drum had sat for fear of obliterating fingerprints or other evidence, Sergio retrieved a shovel from the sheriff 's van. Within minutes, Dorinda's purse, together with a driver's license and other IDs and toiletries thought to have belonged to her, were uncovered and seized. Utilizing his cellphone, he summoned the lab crew from the Sheriff 's department to come and process the scene. He also summoned two of his crack deputies to accompany him when they went to excavate the grave. They were told to get there pronto, and two cruisers with the requisitioned specialists were there within the hour.

While the lab crew processed the scene and with the purse and belongings having been turned over to them, Sergio and his passengers in the sheriff 's van and his deputies in their cruisers followed Crystal as she played the part of the Pied Piper of Hamelin.

Within twenty minutes, Crystal had led her followers to the dump site. Ten minutes later after following an old wagon (now four-wheeler) trail, they were led into a clump of pine trees and the site that would ultimately yield Dorinda's body, the bloody carpet, poker, towels, and Dorinda's clothing.

Crystal had some kind of magical guidance system. It was remarkable and infallible. Whatever invisible force propelled Crystal and her psychic investigation was something Morrey and the others were unable to comprehend. All they knew was that it worked. They thanked God for having given Crystal the mystical power and for having made them the beneficiaries of that power. They were now on their way to ensure that Bruce's charade would be exposed.

• • •

Before Crystal boarded her plane on the return trip to Los Angeles, she advised Morrey and Toby that when she had the vision of Bruce striking Dorinda, she also had a vision of Bruce killing another girl, only that one with a high-powered rifle. She also had a vision of him being acquitted based on a bogus defense. She said that would not happen again. There would be a conviction this time. Crystal then went on to relate that the reason Bruce succeeded the first time around was because the judge had been bought off. She then stated that even though the same judge would initially be appointed on Bruce's next prosecution, he soon would be replaced by "an old, crotchety, take-charge, retired judge."

Surprisingly, she was able to describe the judge in the first trial in precise detail. She referred to him as "Royce" (pronounced Roy-see). Actually, Judge Banyon signed his name as Roy C. Banyon.

She was fairly close. She stated that Royce and Bruce's father were close friends. Bruce's father had given Royce $50,000 the weekend before trial. Both would later claim it was a loan. Crystal then went on to relate that Royce had opened a Denver bank account in his wife's name, where the entire $50,000 was deposited. Royce's wife had been writing checks on that account in increments of $10,000 and depositing the checks in the parties' joint checking account at their Las Cruces bank. Crystal even named the Denver bank.

As they parted, Crystal asked Morrey how he would like living in Denver. When he inquired as to why she was asking the question, she answered by asking one of her own, "Isn't the attorney general required to reside in Denver?"

• • •

By the time the forensics were completed in the death of Dorinda, it was determined that: (1) Dorinda's death was caused by a massive hemorrhaging of the brain resulting from a severe blow to the head; (2) Dorinda's fractured skull was consistent with a blow from the poker found in her shallow grave; (3) Bruce's fingerprints matched the prints lifted from the poker, the oil drum, and tire rim covering the area where Dorinda's purse and toiletries were recovered; (4) the blue belt loop recovered from the cabin where the ring was found matched the blue jeans that Dorinda was wearing at the time her body was recovered; (5) blood recovered from the bed of the trailer that was found in the cabin's outbuilding, the poker, the carpet, and the towels was Dorinda's; (6) the carpet was a match for the fibers recovered from cracks in the floorboards of the area immediately in front of the cabin's fireplace and between the boards on the deck; (7) the dimensions of the carpet matched the dimensions of the darkened area in front of the fireplace; (8) the bloodied towels found buried with Dorinda matched those Sergio confiscated from the cabin; (9) Dorinda was pregnant at the time of her death; and (10) Dorinda's blood-alcohol level was a 0.185.

Dorinda's parents identified her body, even though it was badly decomposed. They also were able to identify her jeans as a pair they had given her on her birthday. The ring found near the bottom cabin step was identified as one given to Dorinda by her paternal grandmother. They also would testify that the last they had heard from their daughter was her call while in transit to the cabin with Bruce. They knew Bruce and recognized his voice and knew it was Bruce who yelled hello into Dorinda's cellphone while they were talking with their daughter. They also would testify as to their visit with Bruce in Fort Collins shortly after Dorinda's disappearance and his story about dropping Dorinda off at the bus station. They also spoke to Dorinda's roommate and confirmed her denial about her ever having summoned Dorinda back to Fort Collins.

In interviewing Dorinda's roommate, she related a conversation she had with Bruce about Dorinda's disappearance. He had told her shortly after returning to school that he had purchased Dorinda's bus ticket back to Fort Collins because of an argument they had over her pregnancy, and he couldn't talk her out of leaving.

There was only one bus company in Las Cruces, and Sergio had already had them check their bookings and was advised by them that Dorinda's name was not on any passenger list either on the day of her disappearance, the day before, or the day after. This was confirmed in writing back in November when Dorinda had first disappeared.

On the basis of the investigation, Morrey filed the following charges against Bruce: first degree murder, tampering with physical evidence, both felonies, abuse of a corpse and concealment of a death, both misdemeanors. A warrant was issued for Bruce's arrest. If he was out of country, as was the rumor, the authorities would need to locate him and attempt to extradite him back. By making the filing and issuance public and Bruce not turning himself in, Bruce would be considered to be a fugitive.

Morrey contacted Montez and advised him of the charges pending against Bruce and of the outstanding warrant. Morrey advised Montez that if Bruce didn't turn himself in, he would consider Bruce's absence interstate flight to avoid prosecution, and if Montez knew where his client was and didn't encourage him to turn himself in, Morrey would consider that the offense of harboring a fugitive. In some respects, Morrey was bluffing and wasn't sure he was on very solid ground. Montez just laughed over the telephone and hung up. However, in less than seventy two hours, with Bruce in tow, Montez entered the district attorney's office.

For some inexplicable reason, the case was assigned to District Judge Roy C. Banyon. Morrey argued that bond should be denied because Bruce had been charged with a capital offense where the proof was evident and the presumption of guilt great. It was, therefore, under state law a non-bailable offense. Judge Banyon nonetheless set bond at $250,000.

Paying the ten percent bond premium to the bondsman, Dr. Spangberg in no time had his son released and back in circulation. By court order, however, Bruce was restricted from leaving the state of Colorado.

Judge Banyon in releasing Bruce was explainable in light of Crystal's revelation concerning Dr. Spangberg's $50,000 so-called loan to Judge Banyon. Morrey wondered how much this one had cost the good doctor. Morrey knew it was just a matter of time before the coconspirators had their day of reckoning—maybe sooner than any of them expected.

CHAPTER 11

Judgment Day

The first degree murder case of *People v. Bruce Spangberg* was on a fast track. Montez filed the usual blizzard of defense motions seeking to suppress evidence, primarily Bruce's statements. Other than the discovery requests, which the prosecution conceded, all of the defense motions were denied. It was speculated that Judge Banyon realized that even if he ruled against the prosecution, the prosecution could and would, prior to trial, appeal those rulings. This was called an interlocutory appeal. So in the quest of liberating Bruce, Judge Banyon would accomplish nothing, as the appellate court could and would overturn and reverse all of Banyon's ill-advised rulings.

There was some urgency in removing Banyon from the case prior to trial. Once the trial commenced and Banyon dismissed the charges, as he had in the first prosecution, the prosecution's appeal would be useless, as Bruce would be deemed to have been placed in jeopardy, and therefore, could not be tried again. With that backdrop, Morrey was back before the grand jury.

Without having to tell Chief Judge Pinkerton T. Calloway the nature of the grand jury probe, Morrey succeeded once again in having Gil Vedder appointed as a special prosecutor and Perry Simms as a special investigator. It would be the same grand jury panel that indicted the errant county commissioners. Morrey detected a glint in Judge Calloway's eyes when he signed the order for appointment of special prosecutor and special investigator.

"Another sensitive matter to present to the grand jury, eh?" was all Judge Calloway said without looking up or expecting a reply.

Back in Las Cruces, Gil and Perry were hard at work preparing for their first judge bribery case. Actually, this assignment was much easier than the last. They had determined through Toby's father, and now chairman of the board of county commissioners, that the Spangbergs banked at the Paraiso State Bank & Trust Co. (PSB&T Co.). Dr. Spangberg had written a lot checks to Milton's business over the years, and there were only two banks in Las Cruces. Through the records at PSB&T Co. they would be able to ascertain on what bank account in Denver the Banyon's checks for deposit had been written.

The grand jury subpoena was issued by Judge Calloway's clerk and directed the custodian of the records at PSB&T Co. to appear before the grand jury and produce the bank account records for both the Banyons and the Spangbergs. Though a little more complicated, the First Centennial Bank & Trust Company, Inc., of Denver was also issued a subpoena requiring their production of the bank records for the account of Josephine Banyon and/or Roy C. Banyon.

• • •

The grand jury was scheduled to meet at two sessions, one week apart. At the first session, the custodians for both the Denver and local bank appeared with the requested records. The Denver bank records showed that Josephine Banyon had opened a bank account with a $50,000 check made payable to her drawn on an account belonging to the Spangbergs. The date of the check? The Friday before Bruce Spangberg's first trial. Nowhere on the check was there a notation that it was a loan. At least $30,000 was subsequently transferred to the Banyon's joint account at PSB&T Co. Records showed that both Josephine and Roy C. wrote checks on that joint account.

Before leaving the stand, the custodian of records for PSB&T Co. presented a check written the past month to Tiller Ford for $28,885 signed by Roy C. Banyon.

As the first session of the grand jury probe into the judge bribery case wound down, a certified copy of that portion of the trial transcript in Bruce's first trial wherein Judge Roy C. Banyon had taken the case away from the jury and directed an acquittal in favor of Bruce was made part of the grand jury record. It included Judge Banyon's bizarre rationale for the ruling to the effect that not one witness could testify that they saw the bullet leave the gun and enter the body. A certified copy of the court record establishing the exact date of the ruling was also presented and made part of the record.

For the following week, Judge Roy C. Banyon, his wife Josephine, Dr. Sydney Spangberg, and Ricardo Tiller from Tiller Ford had been subpoenaed. The grand jury also requested the bookkeeper from Dr. Spangberg's office be subpoenaed to determine whether Judge Banyon was a patient of Dr. Spangberg's.

At the second session of the grand jury probe into the judge bribery case, Ricardo Tiller was called, and he confirmed that Judge Banyon and his wife had purchased a vehicle from his company within the past thirty days and that they had paid by check the sum of $28,885 and that the title had been registered in both of their names. Philicia Reese, the bookkeeper for Dr. Sprangberg's dental practice, testified that Judge Banyon had been a longtime patient of Dr. Spangberg and was Dr. Spangberg's golfing buddy.

Dr. Sydney Spangberg was next called and informed of the nature of the investigation. He was then advised of his Fifth Amendment rights against self-incrimination. Dr. Spangberg stated that he understood but that the whole transaction between the Banyons and himself was innocent and misunderstood. The $50,000 was only a loan and not to influence the judge one way or the other. Since Bruce's case was a jury trial, he didn't think he had done anything inappropriate.

When Gil started to ask questions, Dr. Spangberg immediately proclaimed, "Upon advice of counsel, I respectfully decline to answer upon the grounds that it might tend to incriminate me. I demand my right to immediately confer with an attorney."

Sydney is a wise old fox, Gil thought. *He was able to give his self-serving spiel without having to answer any questions. No wonder he didn't bring an attorney with him; he's already been counseled and rehearsed!*

When Judge Banyon was called, he did something very similar to that of his golfing buddy. He proclaimed his innocence and then invoked his

Fifth Amendment privilege. He parted by saying that his wife was in no way involved in anything and that he was disappointed that the grand jury was resorting to sewer tactics.

It was obvious Josephine Banyon was at wit's end. She was crying before she even entered the grand jury room. Her feeble attempt to invoke her privilege against self-incrimination was honored. She was not a target, and what she would testify to, they already knew. Plus, Gil was familiar with the husband-wife privilege.

Not surprisingly, the grand jurors were quick in returning bribery indictments against both Judge Banyon and Dr. Spangberg. It was a crime for he who confers a pecuniary benefit with intent to influence a public servant and a crime for he who is a public servant to accept a pecuniary benefit in return for the granting of a favor. In Colorado, bribery was a felony carrying a penalty ranging from four to twelve years imprisonment and a fine up to $750,000.

Two of Sergio's deputies had the honor of serving both the briber and the bribee with arrest warrants and copies of the indictments. Both were immediately taken into custody, and with bond having been set at $100,000 for each, both, as expected, bonded out.

Judge Banyon was immediately relieved of his duties and placed on indefinite leave. This meant that the state judicial administrator had to find a temporary replacement. The position was filled by retired Colorado Supreme Court Justice T. Cordell Arnett, sometimes called "Corkey." Judge Arnett was a no-nonsense judge and was heralded by Morrey with great enthusiasm.

• • •

The first Monday in June had been set by the now-defrocked Judge Banyon as the deadline for any plea agreement in the Bruce Spangberg prosecution case, and it was also set as Bruce's bond return date. After his father's indictment, Bruce was nowhere to be found and failed to appear on that first Monday in June. Apparently, he had been frightened away, or perhaps it was the family's way to secrete him and shield him from prosecution. Whatever the reason, his bond was revoked and a bench warrant issued for his arrest. Judge Arnett vacated the trial date that had originally been scheduled for early September. Even if Bruce hadn't boogied, Corkey had a scheduling conflict that would have resulted in the trial date being moved anyway.

• • •

Over the next several weeks, there were a lot of false sightings of Bruce, some as far away as Las

Vegas. One of Dorinda's former classmates told authorities that she thought she saw Bruce in the Alfred Packer cafeteria on the CU campus. One thing was sure: someday, somewhere, he would be found and extradited back to Colorado to face murder charges.

When Morrey lamented the fact that the murder case had been put on hold and would not be tried first, Toby attempted to console him with the positive aspects. "Just think," Toby said, "we can add some new charges such as bond jumping and unlawful flight to avoid prosecution. In addition, since Bruce is a flight risk, it's unlikely he will be allowed to be released on bond when he is captured. His father won't be too happy about forfeiting the $250,000 bond because of Bruce's failure to appear. And we can bolster our case with the flight instruction, which allows the jury to infer that he must be guilty or otherwise he wouldn't have fled the jurisdiction."

"You make me feel better already," said Morrey. "However, if Dr. Spangberg is acquitted on the bribery charge, that might help his son's case."

"Or if Dr. Spangberg is convicted," countered Toby, "that might help our case."

"It does buy us time," admitted Morrey, "to see if more incriminating evidence crawls out of the woodwork."

"Also, the longer Bruce absents himself, the more likelihood Montez will become disenchanted with his client and withdraw."

"Not until his retainer is exhausted," Morrey interjected.

"Good point," said Toby.

• • •

It was summer's end, and Gil, with Perry's help, was geared up for the bribery case against the prominent dentist and the exalted trial judge who sold his soul to the devil for fifty thousand pieces of silver. Gil had a good case, and the defense knew it. Trying to transform a payoff into a loan was something that not even Johnnie Cochran could do. Dr. Spangberg was represented by a Denver attorney by the name of Dinah Carter. A former state prosecutor as well as a former federal prosecutor, Dinah knew her way around the courtroom. Big Bad Banyon was representing himself. The cases had been joined over the objection of both defendants.

Other than the after-the-fact assertions by the two, there was no evidence whatsoever that there was any expectation that the $50,000 would be repaid. When Dr. Spangberg tried to introduce a promissory note in the middle of trial signed by

Big Bad Banyon, it came as a surprise to everyone because it had not been mentioned in the defendants' opening statements. And when Gil produced the owner of a local stationery store on rebuttal who testified he had sold the note form to Dr. Spangberg within the past week, the defendants' house of cards came tumbling down. Now the briber and the bribee, in addition to the bribery charges, would be facing felony perjury charges for manufacturing evidence.

Dr. Spangberg's attorney denied any complicity in the promissory note hoax, and after the guilty verdict was announced and the motion for a dismissal notwithstanding the verdict was denied, Dinah's request to withdraw was granted, and she hightailed it out of the courtroom. After the verdict, the defendants' request that their bonds be continued until sentencing was denied. At sentencing, both Dr. Spangberg and Big Bad Banyon were sentenced to six years imprisonment and each fined $100,000.

Although both appealed their convictions and what they considered cruel and unusual punishment, the same was affirmed by the Colorado Court of Appeals and later by the Colorado Supreme Court. Perjury charges were never pursued in light of the appellate courts' rulings upholding the bribery convictions.

Shortly after the bribery case, Shay Bisben was elevated to district judge and filled the vacancy left by Banyon. Morrey's assistant, Terrence R. Brockerton, filled the county court vacancy left by Judge Bisben. Competency and respectability would once again be the hallmark of the Paraiso County judicial system. The judicial oath of office was a sacred vow that no judge would dare violate again—not here, not now, not ever.

CHAPTER 12

End of the Line

Several seasons had passed, and it was wintertime in Paraiso County. The town was buzzing with the news of Bruce Spangberg's return. It wasn't, however, as he had planned, and this time he was not heralded as a hero. With his tail literally between his legs, wearing a jail orange jumpsuit, and laceless tennis shoes, handcuffs, and ankle shackles, Bruce was led into the courtroom. With long hair and seven months of facial growth, Bruce was unable to hide his hermit past. Being in hiding and coming out only at night, Bruce was pale and gaunt. If it had not been for him loitering and begging in a park adjacent to the bus station in Fargo, North Dakota, he would not have been detained and asked for identification. Being on the run was written all over him, and it was evident the elements had not been kind.

Montez had Bruce cleaned up in rather short order and was able to negotiate more appropriate court garb. Bruce was not able to see much sun locked up in the maximum security unit of the Paraiso County Jail, but jail grub was better than what he had been able to obtain by begging, borrowing, and stealing. Anytime he was out of his cell, he was accompanied by at least two armed deputies and usually handcuffed and shackled.

Bruce had orchestrated his fate as well as that of two young women and maybe even that of his own father, who was now sitting in a prison cell. His disastrous life path was indelibly marked by ruin, devastation, and anguish, and still he had no shame, guilt, or regret. Bruce would not change, with or without the aid of the criminal justice system, and Morrey knew it was his duty to remove Bruce permanently from society. It was not a matter of vindictiveness; it was a matter of duty. At least, Morrey prayed that was his motive.

Morrey did go ahead and file another felony charge on Bruce but would put it on hold pending the outcome of the murder prosecution. The new charge was violation of bail bond conditions. Bruce's nonappearance and leaving the jurisdiction of the state were the basis for the new offense. Ex-judge Banyon hadn't done Bruce a favor by releasing him. Being a capital case where the proof of guilt was evident and the presumption great, it was a non-bailable offense to begin with.

Paraiso County was $250,000 richer and the Spangberg family $250,000 poorer as a result of

Bruce's ill-advised skip. Even though the premium for the bond was ten percent, Dr. Spangberg had posted property, including the cabin property, with the bondsman as security in the event of forfeiture. The bondsman foreclosed, and the infamous cabin now belonged to Catlin Bail Bonds.

When Bruce appeared before Banyon's replacement, there was a whole new atmosphere permeating the courtroom. Bruce was not appearing before an old family friend this time but before a judge who had nothing but disdain for the criminal element. And having presided over the prosecution of the man partially responsible for Bruce's DNA, Judge Arnett, who had remained on this case following his appointment sometime back, knew that bad genes begot bad genes. Any cockiness Bruce may have had upon entering the courtroom faded rapidly the minute the judge's eyes fixed on his.

Even though he didn't realize it at the time, Montez made his first tactical mistake. In seeking to have Judge Arnett excuse, disqualify, and remove himself from the case, Montez only succeeded in alienating himself. Montez argued that because Judge Arnett presided over a case indirectly involving the death of a female victim allegedly at Bruce's hands, the judge would in all likelihood be prejudiced in the pending case involving Bruce in the death of still another female victim. In denying the motion, Judge Arnett, in controlled fury, reminded Montez that, as judge, he was not the trier of fact and that all factual issues would be decided by the jury and that since he was not anxious to be reversed, he would meticulously apply the law. The prosecution team hoped Judge Arnett had a long memory.

The jury trial was scheduled to start promptly at 9:00 a.m. on the ides of March, with counsel on both sides to meet with Judge Arnett in chambers at 8:00 a.m. The clerk would be providing a list of prospective jurors to the attorneys the Wednesday of the preceding week. Montez could have the list e-mailed if he wished. The deadline for any plea disposition would be February fifteenth. The defendant, together with the attorneys, would meet in open court at 9:00 a.m. on that date to handle any disposition and/or any last minute matters.

Morrey and Montez had not previously discussed the alternatives to trial or stipulations that could streamline trial presentation. Montez promised that as soon as he concluded with his client, he would stop by the district attorney's office.

When Montez met with Morrey, Montez did not appear the big bad wolf he had been portrayed. Whether the rumors were exaggerated or because a successful defense was improbable if indeed impossible, Montez was personable and conciliatory. They, however, knew it was virtually an all-or-nothing situation for both. Because of the improbability of a death sentence and the questionable nature of its constitutionality, Morrey's offer to waive the death penalty in exchange for a guilty plea to first degree murder was not particularly alluring to Montez.

"Your offer to waive the death penalty in exchange for a guilty plea to first degree murder would be tantamount to having your cake and eating it too. You wouldn't have to risk an acquittal on the first degree murder charge as you would if you went to trial, and by stipulating to life imprisonment, Bruce in effect would be receiving the same sentence he would likely receive in the event of a conviction anyway. From the defense's perspective, Bruce has nothing to lose by going to trial."

Montez's argument was convincing but there was still the downside. "After killing two innocent girls," countered Morrey, "Bruce is not exactly our community's sweetheart. With Bruce's elaborate deception and cover-up, together with him having fled the jurisdiction, he hasn't exactly endeared himself in the hearts of the citizens of our community some of whom will ultimately be sitting on his jury. I don't think any of them will be that forgiving. I can't believe you or he would be willing to risk all on one roll of the dice."

Morrey would allow Montez no quarter. Montez was backed into a corner but was holding a few cards of his own. "How many times has the Colorado Supreme Court held the death penalty unconstitutional? We both know that Bruce will be old and gray by the time the various appeals wind their way through the criminal justice system, and I'm not as convinced as you are that the good citizens of your community are as eager to impose the death penalty as they once were. This is particularly true where the defendant is barely out of his teen years."

Montez had made his point. Being a seasoned defense lawyer, however, he knew he could not win them all. He also knew it was ill-advised to risk a lot for a little so, being the consonant negotiator that he was, he asked Morrey if he would consider taking a plea of guilty to second degree murder in exchange for a significant sentencing concession.

"Is that a firm offer?" Morrey asked.

"I would have to run it by Bruce and his parents," Montez replied.

"I doubt they would agree," said Morrey.

"Besides, I've already run the possibility of such a plea disposition by my staff and the sheriff's department, and all have scoffed at the idea."

"It appears we have reached a stalemate then," said Montez as he prepared to leave.

Before parting, it was suggested that the two attempt to make stipulations that would make each other's lives more bearable and streamline the rigors of trial. In the next several weeks, they promised they would be in touch with each other.

• • •

When they later spoke by telephone, Montez said he had reviewed the discovery and that his investigator, Justin Prince, had inspected the evidence and interviewed the custodian and all the witnesses who handled each and every piece of evidence. He commended the officers involved in the investigation for their professionalism and said he didn't have any qualms about the prosecution's ability to trace the chain of custody. The defense, therefore, would be stipulating to the chain of custody. He was apologetic, he said, about having subjected the officers to the pummeling at the motions hearing in seeking to suppress evidence, "but it appeared by the way they handled themselves, they were expecting rough treatment." He said by stipulating to the chain of custody, he would not be waiving his objection to the admissibility of evidence on other grounds and would want a continuing objection of those he made at the suppression hearing. Morrey agreed.

Montez said he would waive the production of all the seized items, such as the oil drum, tire rim, blood-stained items, and so on. He would not object to photographs being substituted instead. Morrey said he would still be introducing some of the items themselves but not the bulky ones and appreciated the accommodation.

When Montez said he would stipulate to the qualifications of the forensic experts and not attack their credentials, Morrey realized that Montez was no longer making it a winner take all struggle. Montez would be content if the jury found Bruce guilty of the lesser included offense of murder in the second degree, where intoxication was not a defense. It would be a moral victory for Montez to have Bruce acquitted of the capital offense.

Morrey knew that was the way defense counsel calibrated victory, not by a total and complete acquittal but by an acquittal of the principal charge. The prosecution had been bothered by the recognized defense to first degree murder: intoxication. With Dorinda's blood-alcohol level being at 0.185, as determined by the ME's examination of the vitreous humor in Dorinda's eyeballs, well above the legal limit, it would not be an unrealistic expectation that Bruce's blood-alcohol level would have been as high or even higher. That would mean Bruce couldn't have formed the requisite criminal intent necessary to prove first degree murder. Even his voluntary drunkenness would be a recognized defense. By proving Dorinda's intoxication, the prosecution, in effect, would be proving Bruce's. With Bruce's testimony to that effect and that of a fraternity brother or two, his defense would be established.

Montez' strategy was confirmed when Morrey received the stipulation draft of their telephone conversation together with an additional list of witnesses. Endorsed thereon were the names of Derek Mills, Tinker Poole, and Marianne Mayne together with addresses and telephone numbers for each. The first two had addresses in Fort Collins; the third had a Las Cruces address and telephone number. Morrey had Sergio contact the three. Derek's and Tinker's telephone numbers were the same and were listed to a fraternity house. When interviewed, both vouched for Bruce's erratic behavior when imbibing in and succumbing to alcohol. The third witness was contacted at her place of employment—Las Cruces Liquor Mart. Marianne had gone to high school with Bruce and remembered selling several pints of Black Crow Whiskey to Bruce in the early afternoon the day before Thanksgiving, several days before she read about Bruce's girlfriend's disappearance in the newspaper. She also remembered that even in high school Bruce was a party animal. Bruce's defense was preordained.

When Sergio met with Morrey and Toby, Sergio's dilemma was not the inevitable verdict that would be generated by the intoxication defense but the frivolous nature of going to trial when Bruce was apparently willing to plead guilty to second degree murder.

Morrey said he considered that. "But remember," he added, "there are two charges here. Bruce is also charged with tampering with physical evidence. He wasn't drunk when he committed that offense. That carries a penalty of imprisonment of from one year to a year and a half. That together with a conviction of murder in the second degree, which carries a sentence of from eight to twenty-four years, if run consecutively, would be a minimum of nine years and a maximum of twenty-five-and-a-half years. If the jury returns a guilty verdict to second and not first degree murder and a guilty verdict to the tampering charge, I have a feeling Judge Arnett will think Bruce has already received a break and will sentence him to the max."

"Plus," Toby interjected, "remember what happened the last time we plea bargained a case? The DA's office got a lot of heat."

"Precisely," said Morrey. "Lowering the charges will appear to the public to be a sellout. I can just see Vincenti's letter to the editor: 'Dr. Spangberg bought another one; will our DA never learn?'"

"Is there a downside in not taking a plea to second degree murder other than the adverse public perception?" Sergio asked. "Are we maybe risking a lot for a little?"

"I don't think so," Morrey responded. "It sounds like Montez is throwing in the towel on the second degree murder charge. He knows we have a pretty strong circumstantial case."

"Especially if Bruce takes the stand and says he doesn't remember anything because he was too drunk," added Toby. "That together with his elaborate cover-up and flight will seal his conviction."

"Speaking of the bond-jumping charge," Sergio inquired, "what will happen on that case?"

"Well, since no plea has been entered in that case and we haven't pushed it, speedy trial hasn't yet begun to run. We can wait almost indefinitely, if we need to, to see what happens in the murder prosecution. It's sitting in limbo."

"You two make it sound as though we have no choice but to proceed to trial," Sergio said, shrugging his shoulders.

"I guess it's better for the jurors—the voice of the community—to decide whether Bruce is guilty of first or second degree murder."

"In either case, Bruce will be gone for a long time," said Toby. "It appears Bruce has finally reached the end of the line."

At the last minute, Montez was allowed to file a motion to suppress evidence based on newly discovered evidence. At the hearing, Montez succeeded in obtaining an order requiring the prosecution to disclose the source of their probable cause to search for Dorinda's body and the accompanying incriminating evidence. Upon disclosure of the physic, in essence, as being the source, Montez had a heyday in discrediting the prosecution and their voodoo tactics. If the court granted Montez's motion to suppress, there would be no evidence to convict, and the case against Bruce Spangberg would have to be dismissed.

"Your Honor," Montez began, "maybe we won't need a trial after all. If the prosecution has its way, we can pool our resources and just hire a fortuneteller. Just by looking into her crystal ball, we'll be able to determine the innocence or guilt of Bruce Spangberg."

When Morrey started to object, Judge Arnett beckoned him to remain seated. "This is argument, and both sides are afforded a wide latitude, Mr. Dexter. There is no jury to be prejudiced here. You may continue, Mr. Montez."

Morrey was seething. It was a good thing Judge Arnett hadn't heard what Morrey uttered under his breath.

"This may be the first case in modern history," Montez continued, "where a person was brought to trial on the basis of the magical power of a Shaman. The district attorney's office had not endorsed a psychic or clairvoyant and just recently word had been leaked to us that was how the evidence against Bruce had been obtained. The testimony of a psychic, of course, is not scientifically recognized. If the psychic had been endorsed and called by the prosecution as a witness, his or her testimony would not be allowed. That having been said, evidence obtained through a psychic should likewise be deemed inadmissible. The prosecution should not be allowed to do indirectly what they can't do directly. The physical evidence against the defendant, therefore, should be suppressed."

Navigating his way to the podium wasn't easy.

Morrey's anger hadn't yet subsided, and he knew he had only seconds in which to regain his composure. He silently prayed for divine intervention and inspiration. Only when he was ordered by the judge to proceed was he ready.

"The absurdity of learned counsel's argument is evident," Morrey began. "I wasn't sure I should dignify absurdity with logic and the law but feel compelled to do so."

Clearing his throat and taking a deep breath, Morrey continued, "To counter Bruce's elaborate cover-up, it was necessary to explore every means available to ferret out the evidence in an effort to search for the truth. If it meant utilizing a psychic, so be it. Mr. Montez scoffs at the use of a psychic in this case. Yet, it was the psychic who led us to the victim's grave and the uncovering of the evidence that led law enforcement to the perpetrator, Bruce Spangberg, the defendant in this case. If the defendant had been honest and done the right thing, we wouldn't have needed the services of a psychic. Shouldn't everything be geared toward revelation of the truth? Should that only be the goal of the prosecution or should that also be the goal of the defense and the court?"

With that, Judge Arnett glared over the glasses perched on the bridge of his nose and said, "Mr.

Dexter, it is, of course, always the quest of the court to discover the facts. However, the complaint here is the method by which the prosecution uncovered those facts. Our federal and state constitutions have in place various safeguards the transgression of which is never permitted. The court understands the nature of your argument but is concerned over Mr. Montez's contention that since the methods of a physic are not scientifically recognized then neither should his or her results be recognized. What say you?"

"Your Honor," Morrey quickly responded, "Mr. Montez's argument begs the issue. Here, law enforcement had a legal right to be on the Spangberg property where the body and incriminating evidence was found. This was as a result of permission having been granted to law enforcement by Dr. Spangberg, the owner of the property. Since the search was legal, then the resulting seizure was legal as well. Whether the search was conducted based on a police officer's hunch, the tip of a confidential informant, blind luck, or on the basis of a revelation gleaned from a clairvoyant is irrelevant. It sounds as if Mr. Montez is asking you to throw the baby out with the bathwater."

The ruling of Judge Arnett was not in doubt

until he announced that he was taking the matter under advisement. Usually that was not a good omen. His decision would be announced at 9:00 a.m. the following morning. Morrey, Toby, and Sergio, needless to say, would be experiencing a fretful night.

• • •

Promptly at 9:00 a.m. the Friday before trial, with all the participants present, Judge Arnett announced his decision. "I have agonized over the decision I am about to announce. It was not an easy decision in balancing the rights of the accused against those of society. I do not consider defense's motion to be frivolous or vexatious and spent the better part of last evening researching the case law on the issue. Based on the foregoing and after careful consideration of the facts, the court hereby … denies the defendant's motion to suppress and orders that all parties be present and prepared to proceed to trial this coming Monday at the time previously scheduled. This court will stand in recess until then."

As Judge Arnett banged his gavel signifying adjournment, Morrey turned to Toby with sweat dripping from his brow and under his breath said, "Looks like we dodged another one!"

• • •

At trial, the prosecution through a host of witnesses proved that when Dorinda left in the sole company of Bruce, she was alive. Despite Bruce's conflicting stories, Dorinda never emerged from the mountain. She talked to her parents on the trip up the mountain, and that was the last anyone had heard from her. Bruce's story that he had dropped Dorinda off at the bus station proved false as well as the reason she allegedly had to return to Fort Collins.

When her body was discovered approximately ten miles from the Spangberg cabin, it was badly decomposed. The county coroner nonetheless was able to determine that her death had occurred on or before Thanksgiving Day. The cause of death was attributed to massive hemorrhaging of the brain resulting from a severe blow to the head. A poker found in her shallow grave was covered in Dorinda's blood and was found to be consistent with the instrument used to bludgeon her. The rug and towels from the cabin found with Dorinda's body contained her blood. The oil drum and tire rim concealing the residing place of Dorinda's purse and toiletries in the outbuilding near the cabin bore Bruce's fingerprints. The ring and belt loop found at the bottom of the steps to the cabin were connected to Dorinda. The blood recovered from the bed of the trailer found in the outbuilding near the oil drum and tire rim was determined to be Dorinda's.

Bruce told Dorinda's roommate that the couple argued over Dorinda's pregnancy just before he dropped her off at the bus station. The autopsy revealed that Dorinda was pregnant at the time of her death. When Bruce returned to Fort Collins, he made no effort whatsoever to contact Dorinda or attempt to return the belongings she had left at the Spangberg home in Las Cruces. The clothing she had taken to the cabin was found with her body in the shallow grave.

The prosecution rested its case and Montez made the usual motion for acquittal on the grounds that the evidence was insufficient to sustain a conviction, and therefore the case should not be submitted to the jury but instead should be dismissed. Judge Arnett ruled that there was ample evidence in both quantity and quality to sustain a conviction and denied the motion.

It was now Montez's turn. He had the option of relying on the presumption of innocence afforded every accused or of presenting evidence of his own to create reasonable doubt. He chose the latter.

As his first witness, he called Bruce Spangberg, even though a defendant can never be compelled to testify.

Bruce would have flunked Theatre 101. He made some gestures resembling weeping and some sounds one would make while mimicking a baby in need of its bottle. No tears flowed, and the charade was short lived. Montez followed a script with all questions written out. It was obvious Montez had coached Bruce, and Bruce's testimony was almost too well rehearsed.

"Relate to the jury, please, your full name."

"Bruce Spencer Spangberg."

"Were you in any way involved in the death of Dorinda Sessions?"

Morrey was closely watching Bruce and observed him flinch ever so slightly before answering Montez' question.

"Not that I know of. Both of us had been drinking extensively on our way to my parents' cabin on Stead Mountain, and of course, while we were at the cabin."

"Can you estimate how much the two of you had to drink that Thanksgiving Eve?"

Bruce now appeared to be unflappable and answered without hesitation, "Approximately two pints between the two of us."

"I assume you are talking about alcoholic beverages. What were the two of you drinking?"

"Black Crow whiskey."

"Did the two of you have an argument later that evening?"

"Both of us were pretty drunk, and I don't remember much. I vaguely remember her telling me she was pregnant and us arguing over whether she should have an abortion."

"Do you have any recollection as to whether the argument ever grew violent?"

"I have absolutely no recollection of that. It could have happened, but I was too drunk to remember."

"What do you remember?"

As if reading from a script, Bruce recited, "I just remember waking up in the middle of the night on the kitchen floor and wondering where I was. Everything was foggy, but I remember turning on the front room lights and seeing Dorinda lying on the rug in front of the fireplace. I thought she was asleep, but when I went over to her, I could see blood on the back of her head. When I turned her over and felt for a pulse, there was none. It was then that I realized that Dorinda was dead."

"What did you do then?"

Still sticking to the script, Bruce answered "I panicked and went out to our shed and hooked up a trailer. I rolled Dorinda up in the carpet upon which she had been lying and drug her out onto the front porch and then hoisted her up onto the trailer. I piled some brush on top of her and waited until daylight before I moved her to an old dumpsite some distance from the cabin."

"Did you hear the prosecution's witnesses testify as to where they found Dorinda's body and other items allegedly belonging to her?"

"Yes."

"Who placed those items where they were claimed to have been found?"

"I did."

"Was that after you were sober?"

"Yes."

"Why did you do that and then fabricate the story you told to your parents and later the authorities?"

"To begin with because I was in a daze and later because I was in a panic mode. After Dorinda's death I was not thinking clearly. By the time I came to my senses, I was already over my head in lies."

"Have you told the truth today?"

"Yes, I'm under oath. When I lied about what happened to Dorinda, I was not under oath."

"If you could speak with Dorinda's parents, what would you say to them?"

"I would apologize for having deceived them, and if I was the one responsible for Dorinda's death,

I would ask for their forgiveness."

With that Montez announced that he had no further questions and sat down.

Morrey's cross-examination was not extensive, considering Bruce was now at his mercy.

"When you conceived of your elaborate cover-up scheme," Morrey began, "you had not yet been charged with having murdered Dorinda, had you?"

"No, I hadn't yet been charged."

"Moments ago you admitted that everything you told your parents and the authorities about what had happened to Dorinda were complete falsehoods. Is that your testimony?"

"Yes."

"One of the reasons you lied about your lack of involvement was fear that you might be charged in her death. Isn't that also correct?"

"Yes."

"Now that you are on trial for first degree murder, the stakes are higher than they were before. Wouldn't you agree?"

Bruce shifted in his chair. He was obviously uncomfortable with the questions. "Yes, I suppose so."

"So, if I understand your testimony, when the stakes were lower you lied to save your skin, but here at trial where the stakes are higher you told the truth to save your skin. Is that correct?"

Montez was on his feet objecting and arguing that the question was a mischaracterization of Bruce's testimony as well as being argumentative in nature. Judge Arnett overruled the objection and ordered Bruce to answer.

"Yes, I guess you might say that is correct," Bruce replied.

"You don't deny that when you drove Dorinda to the cabin that she was alive, do you?"

"No."

"You don't deny that the only two persons at the cabin on Thanksgiving Eve were you and Dorinda, do you?"

Bruce glanced at Montez before answering. "No. As far as I know we were the only ones there. After I passed out, I don't know who else may have entered the cabin."

"You don't deny that something or someone caused Dorinda's death on Thanksgiving Eve, do you?"

"No."

"You don't dispute the testimony of the county coroner as to the cause of Dorinda's death, do you?"

"No."

"Would it be fair to say that due to your state of inebriation, you don't know whether or not you were the cause of Dorinda's death?"

"No, I don't know one way or the other if I was the cause of Dorinda's death, and yes, that is a fair statement."

"You don't deny that you were upset with Dorinda over her pregnancy, her failure to disclose the pregnancy to you and refusal to get an abortion and that the two of you had a heated argument, do you?"

"As I stated earlier, I remember her telling me she was pregnant and discussing the possibility of her having an abortion, but the rest is a total blur."

"Come now, Mr. Spangburg, earlier you testified you argued over whether or not Dorinda should have an abortion. Now you call it a discussion. Would you agree there is a difference?"

"I guess."

"To cut to the chase, wouldn't it be fair to say that at the time Dorinda revealed she was pregnant, you became so enraged over her pregnancy, her not having revealed the pregnancy and her refusing to have an abortion that you grabbed the first thing that was handy, the poker near the fireplace, and bludgeoned her to death?"

"As I said, I was too drunk to remember."

"No further questions," Morrey announced. With the unrefuted testimony, Bruce's intoxication was a foregone conclusion. That translated into second degree murder. By his own admission, Bruce was guilty of at least that.

The defense called Bruce's two fraternity brothers who testified as to Bruce's affinity for alcohol and his resulting erratic and unpredictable behavior. Each had their own way of describing Bruce's Dr. Jekyll and Mr. Hyde personality when he drank. The liquor store clerk confirmed Bruce's purchase of alcohol the day he and Dorinda left for the cabin and his affinity for alcohol when he was in high school.

On cross-examination of one of Morrey's forensic experts, Montez had elicited Dorinda's high blood-alcohol reading taken at the morgue. All established the likelihood of Bruce's intoxication at the time of Dorinda's death.

Predictably, the jury returned two guilty verdicts: one to second degree murder and the other to tampering with physical evidence. Montez' attempt to set the verdicts aside and have the judge enter a judgment of acquittal notwithstanding the verdicts fell on deaf and unsympathetic ears. Judge Arnett emphatically denied the motions and punctuated his decision with a loud bang of the gavel. The prosecution, still stinging from Judge Banyon's outrageous ruling in the Torrelli case, heaved a collective sigh of relief when Judge Arnett denied the motion to acquit.

Judge Arnett thereupon ordered a pre-sentence investigation report (PSIR) from the probation department to aid him in imposing sentence. Sentencing was continued to Monday, March twenty-third at ten a.m.

• • •

The morning newspaper was not kind to the Spangbergs. *The Las Cruces Gazette* headline blazed **JUSTICE AT LAST**. The subhead read: **Bruce Spangberg Convicted of Murder**. A rather scathing editorial headlined **End of the Line for Bruce.**

Two of the newspaper's reporters had covered the trial and had reported fairly and accurately. The district attorney's office and local law enforcement at long last were portrayed in a favorable light. Morrey was characterized as having slain the giant referring, of course, to Montez. When interviewed by the press, Montez did, however, claim his share of the victory. After all, his stealth did result in an acquittal of the capital offense, or at least so he claimed.

• • •

At the sentencing, honoring Dorinda's parents' request to address the court, Morrey presented Dr. and Mrs. Emery Sessions. Dr. Sessions did all the talking, as Dorinda's mother was too emotionally distraught to say anything.

"I'm Dorinda's father," Dr. Sessions began. "Standing beside me is Dorinda's mother. Dorinda was our only child. From the day she was born, she was our whole life. We were fortunate to have had such a gifted child. She excelled at everything she did whether it was academics, athletics, or music. She was as beautiful on the inside as she was on the outside. Uncharacteristically, being an only child, she was anything but self-centered. She had a heart of gold and befriended every stray that came her way. One cold winter day when she was nine years old, she came home from school without her new winter coat. She had given it away to a classmate who had no coat. That was our daughter, Dorinda. We couldn't fault her for that gesture of charity."

After comforting his wife who was having trouble controlling her emotions, Dr. Sessions continued, "I'm a medical doctor and was elated when Dorinda came to me just before high school graduation and said she had decided to follow in my footsteps and become a medical doctor. She said the two of us could practice medicine together." It was now Mrs. Sessions turn to comfort her husband.

After regaining his composure, Dr. Sessions continued, "Every parent wants his or her child to be happy. We rejoiced at Dorinda's professed love for a fellow student. His name was Bruce Spangberg. She shared with great enthusiasm and joy the dreams she had for the two of them. Dorinda was madly in love with Bruce, and her face glowed whenever she talked about him." Hesitating momentarily, Dr. Sessions then stated: "I don't know what went wrong on that mountaintop. Both Dorinda's mother and I have been praying that God's will would be done in the imposition of Bruce's sentence. We place Bruce's fate in the hands of he who gives life." With that, Dr. Sessions led his grieving wife to their seat on the other side of the court railing.

Morrey, thinking of his own two daughters, put himself in the Sessions' place and fought the urge to cry. He admired their faith and wondered if he could be so generous.

Montez' witnesses in mitigation of sentence had been carefully selected and were unabashed in their plea of clemency for Bruce. The first was a former high school teacher of Bruce's.

"My name is Jonathan Hartshorn. Bruce was one of my former students at Central High School. I guess I would describe Bruce as a promising student with a great future. He was popular, talented, and a good athlete. He was hardworking and never caused problems. It's my opinion that

Bruce should be placed on probation as prison would be counterproductive. I feel Bruce has learned a valuable lesson from all of this and will not reoffend."

The next witness was Bruce's minister. Not unlike Mr. Hartshorn, Reverend Paul Mendenhall was also convinced that Bruce should not be incarcerated.

"I'm Reverend Paul Mendenhall, Bruce's minister. I have known Bruce and his family for over fifteen years. Although I haven't seen Bruce much since he went away to college, I do see him when he returns home from time to time. As far back as I can remember, Bruce was a fun-loving kid involved in various charitable and community projects. I recall a time when just Bruce and I repaired and painted a dilapidated house for an elderly handicapped woman. I also remember when Bruce and several of his friends helped with the distribution of turkeys to the less fortunate on several Thanksgivings, including the Thanksgiving of his first year of college."

After clearing his throat, Reverend Mendenhall continued, "I too am in favor of probation. That way, Bruce would be able to pay his debt to society by useful community service, and thereby both he and the community would benefit. Bruce clearly is repentant, and I'm of the opinion that he has learned his lesson and will never be back in court again."

The last person called by the defense in mitigation of sentence was Bruce's mother, Serena. She was not at all intimidated by the court proceedings, and in fact, was eager to address the court. As a former junior high school teacher, she brought a crispness that only a school teacher could. Abrupt and to the point, she decried a system that would transform two misadventures into criminal events.

"I'm Bruce's mother and am here to speak in his behalf. To begin with, this whole episode has been blown way out of proportion. My son's motives have been totally misconstrued, and having known him all his life, I can categorically tell you that he is not the monster the criminal justice system has painted him to be. Frankly, I'm surprised the jury in this case was not like the judge in the previous case and didn't see the case for what it really was. In fact, the word *surprised* might not be the right word. I should probably say, I was *shocked* by the verdict. To treat my son as a coldblooded killer is a travesty in light of all the violent offenders out there running free. A sentence to a prison term would be outlandish and would only add to the list of victims in this case, if we could call them that."

Bruce's mother paused for a moment and then added, "The kids were drinking and shouldn't have been, and no one knows for sure what really happened on that mountain. What appeared to happen was unfortunate, but two wrongs don't make a right." After catching Bruce's eye, she abruptly made her way back to her seat.

With parents like the Spangbergs always covering for him, no wonder Bruce turned out to be a monster, thought Morrey.

Judge Arnett then asked Montez if he wanted to be heard. He acknowledged he did and walked to the podium. He then stated: "Bruce's former high school teacher, minister, and mother know Bruce better than I do or anyone else in the courtroom. However, from my familiarity with the case and having discussed Bruce with numerous individuals, Bruce's involvement was an enigma and an aberration. It certainly was out of character. A prison sentence, as recommended by the probation department, is not warranted under the circumstances and would only result in removing an otherwise productive member from society. To sit in a prison cell would be a total waste, particularly when a segment of the community could derive a benefit from Bruce's charitable endeavors."

Montez then argued, "For the foregoing

reasons, I oppose the recommendation of the probation department and propose that Bruce be placed on probation in lieu of a prison term, and that as a condition of probation, he be required to perform a significant amount of useful public service. That way the community would be spared the heavy cost of incarceration, would benefit in a positive way, and Bruce would be better able to pay any fine that might be imposed."

When Judge Arnett addressed Morrey, he asked if the district attorney's office opposed the recommendation of the probation department. Morrey announced that the district attorney's office concurred with the recommendation of imprisonment. When next asked if he had anything to say, Morrey positioned himself at the rostrum, and pausing only briefly, began: "May it please the court. Bruce may be an enigma and an aberration to Mr. Montez, but not to our community and especially not to the families of Sandra Torrelli and Dorinda Sessions. There is not just one, but two young women who will not realize their dreams because of the improvident acts of the defendant. My heart goes out to the defendant's mother for having to face the prospect that her son will end up in prison. But she will be able to speak with and to her son after court today and in the days to come, whether he is imprisoned or not. He will not be locked up forever, and there will come a day when mother, father, sister, and son will be reunited and will not have to wait for eternity to do so.

"Neither today after court nor any other day will Dorinda's parents, brothers, sisters, relatives, and friends nor Sandra's parents, brothers, sisters, relatives, and friends be able to speak to or with either of them. And in twenty-five years or less, when Bruce returns to his parents, sister, relatives, and friends, there will be a reunification. Not so with the Sessions or the Torrellis. They will have to await a distant time, a distant place, and a different realm to see their loved one again.

"It doesn't seem fair that the innocent should suffer for the senseless acts of another. Society is not seeking an eye for an eye or tooth for a tooth. The sentence here is not a trade-off of a death of one for the death of two. Bruce's life has been spared with the acquittal on the first degree murder charge, and the harshness of the alternative prison sentence he could have received if convicted of that charge has also been shortened. His intoxication has already been factored in; he has received his break—a break his innocent victims didn't receive when he was making the decisions.

"The defendant's calloused attitude and

willful disregard of all decency was exemplified by his sober and deliberate acts the days following Dorinda's death. The disposal of her body and personal effects, deceiving her family and friends and even his own family, and carrying on as if nothing happened are not acts of someone who is concerned for others. He was and is concerned only for himself and what is in his own best interest. If Dorinda's remains had not been uncovered by law enforcement, Bruce would still be perpetrating the great deception. He was not moved by his sinister acts then, and he certainly isn't now. The only remorse he has is that he got caught. Even the maximum sentence Your Honor can impose is too good for Bruce Spangberg."

Judge Arnett then had Bruce stand. Bruce was then asked if he had anything to say in his own behalf before sentencing was imposed. Whether for noble reasons or contrived to save his own skin, Bruce just sobbed, this time shedding real tears. Uncontrolled and shaking, he was joined on one side by his attorney and on the other by his mother.

Bruce received twenty-four years, the maximum on the murder charge, and one year on the tampering charge. The sentences were ordered to run consecutively. The twenty-five-year sentence would be served at the Colorado State Penitentiary in Canon City, the same facility in which Bruce's father was incarcerated. All that appeals thereafter would accomplish was further dissipation of the family cache.

• • •

After the guilty verdict was announced, Toby turned to Morrey and whispered, "Crystal was right on."

Morrey just nodded. He now pondered another of her predictions. Someday, she said, Morrey would be the attorney general of the state of Colorado, or at least that was what she inferred. Dispelling the thought, Morrey knew he still had a lot of unfinished business in Paraiso County. But for now, he would be content in knowing that Bruce Spangberg had reached the end of the line.

CHAPTER 13

A Drug Deal Gone wrong

Melanie Marley had been in and out of the criminal justice system since the eighth grade. She had come from a fairly well-to-do family and being an only child, she had access to what appeared to be a limitless supply of greenbacks. With the financial backing of her parents and her unusual good looks and charm, she was able to avoid any felony convictions. Once she got hooked on meth, however, all that changed.

At age twenty, Melanie ended up with her first drug conviction. Everything went downhill from there. In and out of rehab, she finally ended up in the big house. There she met two meth addicts, Courtney Faust and Delores Dollen. Courtney of late was from Boulder and Delores from Colorado Springs. Both were military brats, and both shared drug histories similar to Melanie's.

The prolonged use of meth and occasionally other illegal substances had taken their toll on the three. With their natural attributes dissipated, they learned to become cruel, cunning, and shrewd. Since Melanie was older than the other two, she became the ringleader. They fed off each other and the three as a unit became a formidable force to reckon with. They referred to themselves as the *Indestructibles*. The Women's Correctional Facility became the birthplace of what would later be referred to as *the grand scheme*.

• • •

Melanie was released first and returned to Paraiso County, residing on a large cattle ranch homesteaded by her great-great grandfather and now operated by her parents. Within the year, both Courtney and later Delores were released from the correctional facility. As per their jailhouse prearranged plan, they teamed up with Melanie and were provided a large bunkhouse which they made their home on the Marley Ranch.

Having been coached by other seasoned inmates at the correctional facility, the girls implemented the advice their mentors bestowed on them and were careful not to purchase their supplies in Paraiso County. They were educated on how to set up an elaborate methamphetamine manufacturing plant and did so on the most isolated and camouflaged area of the Marley Ranch. Their lab was state-of-the-art, and there they cooked their way to stardom.

Melanie's father thought Melanie and her

guests might be growing marijuana and maybe even some illegal mushrooms but never suspected the girls were operating their own private meth lab. The operation was well-conceived, and with the gerrymandered version of the catalytic converter, an ingenious device for which they could easily have obtained a patent, their manufacturing plant was most efficient, and because of its location, was virtually undetectable.

The Indestructibles had built an alliance with Melanie's old high school sweetheart, Morano Balkin. Morano had spent some time in Canon City, as had his underlings, Packie Erickson and Boyce Carsten. Morano's father had been a small-time gangster in Paraiso County for a number of years. Right after Sergio was elected sheriff, Mercury Balkin just disappeared and hadn't been seen or heard from since. There was some speculation that his burial place was at the bottom of the cement that lined the Olympic-sized swimming pool at City Park. Who may have snuffed him out, nobody knew for certain.

Upon their arrival, Melanie had introduced Courtney to Packie and later Delores to Boyce. Melanie started dating Morano again, and the three couples, looking angelic, sat together in church on Sundays. They were lauded for their miraculous transformations and for having overcome their drug addictions. They were active in various service clubs, involved in community fundraising projects, and all were members of the Las Cruces Chamber of Commerce. The community was most forgiving and understanding. Everybody makes mistakes in their lives, but not everyone learns from their mistakes. Here were the three couples who pulled themselves up from their bootstraps and were making something out of their lives. They were to be commended, not condemned. Each was certainly in line for the citizen-of-the-year award.

• • •

The community was stunned when Melanie's bullet-riddled body was found in the alley behind an abandoned warehouse on the outskirts of Las Cruces. To Sergio's deputies who discovered Melanie's body, it was obvious she had been killed execution-style. It was a type of killing found in old Chicago newsreel clips and modern-day gangster films but not an occurrence with which the locals were familiar—at least not within the last one hundred years.

Morano Balkan seemed the most distressed over Melanie's death. Whether retreating into a shell of grief or into hiding, it wasn't apparent. Whatever the reason, Morano dropped from sight. The same thing was true of his sidekicks and the remaining Indestructibles. The community was buzzing with speculation, and there was a plethora of outlandish rumors. None, however, involved drugs and especially not methamphetamines.

• • •

Gorman Hedge, a former FBI agent and now the head of the DEA taskforce out of Denver, contacted Morrey. He was headed for Las Cruces and wanted to talk to Morrey. When Hedge arrived at the DA's office, Toby and Sergio were waiting with Morrey in the conference room. A rather unimposing bespectacled, middle-aged man with a full head of thick, gray hair and matching mustache entered and introduced himself as "Gore."

Gore then went on to relate a scenario that boggled their minds.

"Paraiso County," Gore began, "has become the well-spring of one of the largest drug operations in the United States, with international connections. The feds have been working on trying to infiltrate the organization for almost two years and have only penetrated the epidermis. The death of Melanie Marley is connected to our investigation, and Ms. Marley was thought to be the kingpin, or should I say the Queen Pin or Queen Bee."

Morrey, Toby and Sergio sat listening in utter

disbelief. It was obvious by their expressions that their ignorance of the whole affair was a reflection of their feeling of incompetence. They remained silent and frozen in their chairs.

Gore went on to explain, "The main characters in this operation and its heart and soul are or were three couples each made in the image and likeness of Bonny and Clyde. They are or were residents of your jurisdiction, and all are or were ex-cons and drug addicts. I'm sure you either know them or know of them. I say were because, as I have said, one of the key players has recently been eliminated. Starting at the top of the hierarchy, was Melanie Marley and then Morano Balkin, Courtney Faust and Packie Erickson, and then Delores Dollen and Boyce Carsten."

A red-faced Sergio glanced at Morrey and Toby. "Right under our noses," he said disgustedly.

"Don't beat yourselves up over this," Gore said. "They were as cunning and shrewd as they come. The six were the sole shareholders of a Colorado corporation known as Mel-Mor Corporation, Inc. (M-MCI). Melanie was the president, and Morano was the treasurer. Basically, Melanie was the CEO; Morano the CFO. Melanie and Morano collectively owned fifty-one percent of the stock; the remaining forty-nine percent was divided between the other four. The corporation is what the business world would term a vertically integrated firm. M-MCI was involved in the entire chain of production of a product that was and is illegal to produce, specifically methamphetamines.

"Our sources tell us that the product is manufactured or produced in Paraiso County, and the exact location is thought to be Melanie's father's ranch. Although we have taken some aerial photographs, our equipment has not detected the exact location. There is an old wagon trail that shows a lot of heavy recent travel leading to a location where an old cabin sits in a thicket of tall pines near the Wyoming-Nebraska border. Surveillance photographs have detected smoke from time to time but not enough to get a search warrant. And we've been very careful not to send in a ground crew from the Wyoming-Nebraska side for fear of blowing our cover and alerting anyone before we can make the bust.

"M-MCI's operation is from the cradle to the grave. It's involved not only in the manufacturing phase but the transportation, distribution to wholesalers, and sale to retailers phases as well. It doesn't sell directly to consumers and has deliberately insulated itself not only from the consumers, but the retailers as well. The only ones who seem to know who's pulling the strings are the wholesalers. Also, the product is not distributed locally, and as part of M-MCI's franchise agreement with the wholesalers, the wholesalers are prohibited from selling to retailers in your county or directly to citizens and residents of Paraiso County.

"They now have distributorships not only in Colorado but in five other western states: Wyoming, Utah, Arizona, Nevada and California, with plans to expand into Idaho, Oregon, and Washington. Although we haven't been able to verify it, our sources tell us there are now franchises located in Canada."

Interrupting Gore for the moment, Morrey, still stunned by the revelation, commented, "It certainly is strange that red flags haven't been raised in the business community, such as among the suppliers of raw materials that are the ingredients needed to make the meth, the banks where their funds no doubt are being funneled, the tax people, and so on."

"It's quite simple, frankly," said Gore. "M-MCI has been careful not to purchase its supplies locally and never a lot from just one outlet. The rest is a bit more complicated. M-MCI has set up an investment holding company in the Cayman Islands close to Jamaica. The reason I mentioned Jamaica is because the holding company is called

Jamaica International Enterprises, Ltd. (JIEL). All the stock in M-MCI, cash, and other investments have been transferred to JIEL.

"The offshore jurisdiction offers not only tax benefits to the M-MCI shareholders but diverts the government's attention away from the accumulation of funds and the eyebrow-raising transactions in which M-MCI engages. Up to this point, M-MCI has been creative in funneling those funds back to the US. Theoretically, it is required to report and pay taxes once the profits are brought onshore, but thus far, it has been able to circumvent the law, and that may be its undoing. The IRS has had their investigators working on the case for some time now and apparently are fairly close in the prosecution of M-MCI and those connected with it on fraud and tax evasion charges."

"You haven't explained how Melanie Marley's death figures in all of this," Sergio interjected.

"Yes, that's also a long, involved story. The three couples spent a lot of time in Denver setting up their business and recreating. Their favorite place to relax was Sallan's Sport Bar in Brighton. There, they met and became fast friends with Tony Sallantini and his wife, Marietta. Tony and Marietta are in their early sixties and hail from Chicago. When Tony's father had been assassinated by a mob rival, Tony,

Marietta, and their now-grown children moved to Colorado to lay low. Ultimately, they moved to the Denver area and opened the sport bar.

"The main distributor for M-MCI had been Morano and his cousin, Marco Balkin. Marco was a native of Denver whose occupation was listed as a professional gambler. To pay off his gambling losses and support his heavy drug habit, Marco had been dealing drugs. When approached by Morano to be an outlet for the newly manufactured meth, Marco, at first, was enthusiastic about the opportunity and undertook the task with much zeal. Marco, however, began siphoning off the drugs to satisfy his own habit, and feeling his share of the profits was unfair, began dipping in the till. This caused tension between the two cousins. So when Tony made a proposal, Morano jumped at the chance.

"Tony is a tough guy who has been involved in some rather shady deals and always wants to make a quick buck. He was named after his grandfather, who reputedly obtained his name when his mother, Morano's great grandmother, upon sending her son to America, used a grease pen to mark her son's forehead with the destination *to New York*. However, she abbreviated New York. Upon his arrival in the New World and until he was killed in a barroom fight, he was known as 'ToN.Y.,' or simply Tony.

"Morano had to cut a fat deal with Tony and agree to an exclusive franchise. The franchise became an instant moneymaker. M-MCI's take was almost twenty times what it had been under Cousin Marco. Tony had a *family* and a team that accounted for his success. Unfortunately, blood was thicker than water, and Morano couldn't keep the ties with Tony, and having made up with cousin Marco, the two began operating on the side undercutting Tony's operation. Predictably, Tony found out. When Marco was confronted by one of Tony's family members, Marco denied the arrangement. It took persuasion, but the truth ultimately emerged. The confrontation precipitated an act of violence that resulted in Marco's death. One of Tony's *family*, it was determined, was a police informant.

"When Morano found out about Marco's death, he went looking for Tony. When Morano, Packie, and Boyce entered Sallan's Sport Bar armed for combat, Tony was nowhere to be found. Actually, upon being warned by his manager, Tony reputedly had slipped out a back door. Morano made a scene in front of staff and customers and threatened he would be back, and upon seeing Marietta, told her she better get used to being a widow, as her husband would soon be history.

"Apparently upset over himself for not having

stayed to face the music and for having subjected his wife to the abuse intended for *him*, and apparently still upset over Morano's double-cross, Tony commissioned one of his lieutenants to teach Morano a lesson—one Morano wouldn't forget. Unfortunately, we have no evidence to bridge the gap. We can only assume Tony was responsible for Melanie's death. Although we can't prove it, putting together bits and pieces, we're led to believe there are others in Tony's crosshairs. Definitely Morano, and maybe Packie and Boyce as well. To make Packie and Boyce suffer as had Morano, we would not be surprised if the next two bodies you find will be those of Courtney and Delores.

"Because of the complexities of the drug investigation and the extensive nature of the operations, we will need witnesses who are insiders, otherwise we will be operating in the dark. The cancer has permeated the whole body, and yet all we can see is a mole. For one thing, we need to locate and confiscate the factory. For another thing, we need to identify all those in the distribution network and cut off the dragon's head. Otherwise, illegal drugs will find their way into the hands of more school kids and those whose lives will never be the same again if we don't."

"What do you want from us?" asked Morrey.

"Not what you think," Gore responded. "We want you to stay out of it and let the DEA and the feds do their job."

"That won't be easy for us to do," said Sergio. "I assume at some point you'll want us to become involved."

"If you've known this all along, why haven't you contacted us sooner?" asked Toby.

Before Gore could answer the question, Morrey chimed in, "How will we know the strangers in town are DEA or feds and not hit men bent on revenge?"

"One question at a time, please," replied Gore. "To answer the last question first, we'll introduce you to the state and federal agents. We want you to know who they are and for them to know who you are. To answer Sergio's and Toby's questions, we would like to involve you from time to time and have you handle various assignments. However, too many chefs can spoil the soup. Also, our agency is involved in the total investigation, and Paraiso County is only one segment although, admittedly, maybe the most important. With the distribution system they have in place, even if the Paraiso County sources should dry up, they undoubtedly can find alternative sources. It's the wholesalers and street traffickers with whom we are most concerned right now."

Being satisfied with Gore's reasoning, Morrey stated, "You have our pledge of complete cooperation and support. We'll keep our eyes and ears open and will keep you informed. We assume you will do the same with us."

"Absolutely," Gore promised. "If the rat, namely Morano Balkin, emerges from his hole, you might keep an eye on him. I have a feeling that's where the action will be found."

• • •

Although it hadn't taken long to locate Morano, he didn't emerge from his hole—at least not alive. The frantic voice on the other end of the 911 call was that of a Shelley Windsor. Her boyfriend of only two months had accidentally been shot, and an ambulance was urgently needed. Upon arrival, the EMTs contacted a young woman in her mid-to-late-twenties. She was in a bathroom and crying hysterically. She pointed to a bedroom where a man in his mid-forties, clad only in his shorts, lay face up on a king-sized bed. His eyes were bulging, his mouth gapped, and his head covered in blood. He couldn't be resuscitated. They noticed an entrance wound to the temple and a revolver on the floor not far from the bed.

Since the death scene was located in the

county, two sheriff 's investigators arrived along with Sergio. The EMTs had not moved the body. Shelley was now sitting on a chair positioned close to the bed, and was still crying hysterically. She was ultimately removed to another room and there told Sergio and the two deputies an unbelievable story.

Shelley had met Morano in a local club. He was with two friends and their girlfriends. Even though she was there with a date, Morano asked her to dance. When he did this several more times, she relented and her date thereupon became disgusted and left. She ended up going home with Morano and from then on would spend a lot of time with him after work and on weekends. She was a cosmetologist and had her own shop. The only times she saw Morano leave his home was the night they met and on one occasion when she cut his hair in her shop.

She said Morano seemed preoccupied and depressed. He was grieving over someone who had recently died, and he refused to talk about it. Although he never took drugs in front of her, she knew he was taking drugs because of his mood swings. Several times he became morbid and talked about crossing over to the other side. She knew he had visitors while she was at work because she would find dirty cups, glasses, silverware, plates and other evidence indicating the presence of others. She assumed they were the two friends and their girlfriends who had been with him the evening they met.

This night, she said, Morano seemed high and was fooling around with a revolver she had never seen before. She didn't know anything about guns, and Morano showed her how it operated. He showed her how to load and unload the revolving cylinder. He emptied cartridges into a drawer in the nightstand next to the bed and showed her how to check to make sure there were none in the cylinder. They then proceeded to pull the trigger, pretending to shoot at various targets around the room and then ultimately at each other. All this was done after they readied themselves for bed and were lying in bed. They continued the regimen while they watched a movie on television.

While the commercials were aired, Shelley went into the bathroom. When she returned, Morano was still playing with the revolver. When she repositioned herself on the pillow propped behind her and next to Morano, he handed her the gun and said, "Pretend to shoot me."

Helping her put the gun to his head, she pulled the trigger. The unexpected bang and repercussion caused the revolver to fly out of her hand and off the edge of the bed and her with it. In the process, she saw Morano's head explode, an image she said was indelibly etched in her memory.

While Shelley dressed, the two investigators, who were crime scene analysts, began processing the scene. For now, it would be treated as a crime scene. Worried about Shelley's mental condition, Shelly was transported to Mercy Hospital where she was given some sedatives and confined by the doctor on call until the next morning. Before Morano's body was transported to the morgue, both Morrey and Toby were called. Both arrived, and viewing the body, ordered an autopsy.

• • •

Early the following morning, Gore was notified of Morano's death. Gore said he wanted to be present when Shelley was interviewed. At 10:30 a.m. sharp, with Morrey, Toby, Sergio, and Gore present, Shelley was interviewed. Even with the passage of time and the medication, Shelley was a basket case. She was upset with herself for not having checked the cylinder and for having participated in such a dangerous game. She did not try to pass the blame onto her lover.

After an extensive interview, Shelley was sent out of the room. Gore told the others he just wanted to make sure Morano's death was accidental. He did not see Tony's signature on the shooting. He indicated the DEA would be doing a background check on Shelley. He then determined from Sergio that Shelley had no criminal record and was not involved in drugs. He recommended that Shelley still be polygraphed. Sergio had a polygrapher from the CBI that he would use and possibly have the task completed by the end of the day. By the close of the day, Gore was notified that Shelley showed no deception. She had passed the polygraph. The shooting was an accident.

In the old days, Shelley would have had to submit to the Tarugo Polygraph to be tested. The one she took today was not as invasive. She appeared to be relieved when she was informed that no criminal charges would be filed against her. Her situation was considerably different than the first Spangberg case where the shot was fired deliberately into the bathroom door, killing an innocent girl. Though her conduct was careless and should not be tried at home, it did not, in Morrey's view, rise to the level of criminally negligent homicide. All felt he exercised his prosecutorial discretion wisely in this instance. If there were detractors, he was not so informed.

• • •

After Morano's death, nothing happened out

of the ordinary the next two months, and then all hell broke loose. While on their way to the Marley Ranch with Packie Erickson and Courtney Faust in the front seat and Boyce Carsten and Delores Dollen in the backseat, the four were ambushed by two of Tony's executioners. When Packie parked his SUV behind the old white van stalled in his lane, and while stepping out onto the roadway to see what was amiss, Tony's boys opened fire with their semi-automatics. Even though armed, Packie was fatally wounded. However, as Packie was falling, he was able to pull his weapon and got off one shot, the only shot fired by the ambushees. Call it luck, fate, or divine providence, the shot struck the van's gas tank, and instantly the ambushers were toast—make that burnt toast. That made a half-dozen new customers for the undertaker and six less criminals for the authorities to prosecute.

Gore was not very pleased when he surveyed the cookout. Dead men or women don't talk. There weren't enough pieces to complete the puzzle, and the worst was there was no one alive to tell the authorities where to look for the missing pieces. Tony could provide some pieces, but even if they could get him to talk, the pieces he would provide would by design be pretty insignificant.

When asked about how valuable the police

informant would be in at least convicting Tony, Gore replied that the informant's dismembered body had been discovered in a dumpster several days before, and there were signs that he had been tortured and ceremoniously executed. Tony had a way of getting people to talk and then silencing them forever. The feds were back to square one as far as Tony was concerned.

• • •

Melanie's father was more than willing to let the DEA agents search the Marley Ranch. Finding the elaborate meth lab and utilizing reverse engineering, they were able to learn the secrets of the improvised catalytic converter. It was an ingenious device that even had the experts scratching their heads. Gore personally supervised the destruction of the lab itself because, as he phrased it, "its advanced technology was truly a trade secret, and if it found its way into the wrong hands, could have disastrous results."

"If only Melanie had used her extraordinary talents for the betterment of mankind," her father kept mumbling, "she would still be with us, and we would be praising her instead of burying her."

The role played by local law enforcement in Paraiso County in the war on meth was fairly insignificant. The manufacturing plant operating right under their noses was like the Trojan horse left at the gates of Troy. Its unsuspecting nature made the county vulnerable to destructive forces for which the county was totally unprepared to overcome or conquer. Forewarned is forearmed. Hopefully, the lesson learned would make law enforcement more vigilant and would allow them to close the barn door before the horse bolted. This time they dodged a bullet; next time, they might not be so lucky.

LICENSE TO CONVICT — CARROLL MULTZ

CHAPTER 14

The Moment of Truth

Morrey's third term was passing in a flash. With only six months left of his term, he knew there would not be a fourth. Recently, he had even been second-guessing himself about the precipitous decision to run for the third term. When the legislature set a two-term limit on district attorneys, they had a reason. That restriction could be and was overridden by his district's voters and hence the reason Morrey was able to seek the third term. *One term too many*, he lamented.

He prayed for guidance as his once reliable compass seemed to have stopped functioning. He wasn't panicked about what he was going to do, but he certainly was apprehensive. Maybe the word was anxious. Although they meant basically the same, Morrey preferred apprehensive over anxious, as anxiety was classified by his old psychiatrist hunting and fishing buddy as an abnormality.

Perhaps this was not a good time to be circumspect in light of his turbulent stint in the district attorney's office, and in particular, the events of the past several months. It was like shopping in the grocery store at the end of a long day when you only had a bowl of soup for lunch. You might be making error-ridden decisions that you would later regret. Nonetheless, Morrey was resting his eyes and staring out his office windows at the majestic Rocky Mountain Range with snow still on the peaks this clear, crisp day in May. The pages marking the days on his desk calendar were being flipped much too rapidly, and Morrey was wondering where the last eleven-and-one-half years had gone. Theresa would be seventeen by the start of her senior year in high school, and Julia would be fifteen and starting her sophomore year. He and Monique would be thirty-nine by year's end. His mother was pushing sixty-five.

When he shaved that morning, Morrey's reflection in the mirror reminded him of a portrait of his father that he had hanging in his home study. When his father was in his thirties, Morrey thought his father was old. When he died, he was younger than Morrey's current age. Life is certainly fleeting and unpredictable, Morrey thought. The only thing that is predictable is one's death. Everyone was born with an expiration date, and that was bothering Morrey. He wished he knew what his expiration date was. He could call Crystal, but then again, maybe it was best he didn't know.

In some ways, he envied Crystal for her ability to form psychic impressions of the past and of things yet to come. Just knowing what path to take and what decisions to make would avoid a lot of mistakes and unnecessary detours and dead ends. When he first became district attorney, he was decisive and intuitive. Now he was revisiting many of those decisions and second-guessing himself. Whereas in the past he might have been wrong but never in doubt, he was now convinced he was wrong even when he wasn't. Dauntless in his early undertakings as a district attorney, Morrey was finding himself addressing challenges with fearful uncertainty.

Recently, Morrey had been agonizing over prosecutorial decisions for which he had been criticized in the press. Although he had been taught to ignore the detractors, as there would always be some, he still was troubled. Recrimination was something with which he had never really learned to cope. He was eager to please everyone even as a child and particularly now when he wanted to leave office on a high note.

• • •

One particularly troublesome recent case was the granting of a deferred judgment and sentence to Fenton F. Dillman.

Dillman was a self-professed investment

adviser from Cheyenne. His credentials were questionable, but nonetheless he was able to convince a significant segment of the elderly across the Colorado line to invest with him. He offered them investment opportunities that they thought were too good to be true. And it turned out more often than not that they were too good to be true. Many lost their life savings investing in Dillman's hair-brained investments. Dillman made a good living off the front-end investment fees and the back-end commissions. He always was one step ahead of the law and skated dangerously close to criminal prosecution on more than one occasion.

Edna Maddox was a retired librarian and living in Las Cruces. Now in her eighties, she had been a client of Dillman's for a number of years and was one of the fortunate ones to have benefited from Dillman's investment advice. She had no complaints about that. However, when she had accumulated $10,000 that was sitting around doing nothing, Dillman agreed to invest it for her. Commingled with the hundred $100 bills were twenty-five $100 bills issued by the state of Colorado in the 1800s which had been left to her by her grandfather. Because of their antiquity, they were worth a king's ransom. When Dillman discovered them, he substituted them with twenty-five contemporary $100 bills. When Edna discovered her error, she demanded return of the antique bills. Dillman denied he had received them. Only through interviewing a coin collector in Cheyenne was law enforcement able to prove that Dillman had converted the bills to his own use. Fortunately for Edna, Dillman, without prompting, retrieved and returned the bills.

Dillman had committed fraud on the elderly. Actually, Edna was classified as an at-risk adult. Morrey had the option of filing charges under one of two Colorado statutes. Both were felonies. After filing criminal charges, Edna refused to cooperate and wanted the charges dropped. Not wanting to drop the charges completely, Morrey worked out an arrangement with Dillman's attorney, whereby Dillman would enter a guilty plea pursuant to a deferred judgment and sentence, meaning that the guilty plea would be held in limbo for a period of two years, and if Dillman fulfilled all the terms and conditions of the agreement, he could withdraw his plea and the case would be dismissed.

As might be expected, Edna was not happy with Morrey for pursuing the case. The public, on the other hand, was not happy that the DA plea bargained still another case. The press, of course, exacerbated the situation and made it a political football. Par for the course, Morrey thought as he recounted the whole incident.

• • •

Another controversial decision he was pondering was one involving the high school girls' track coach. A seventeen-year-old girl who was one of Theresa's classmates claimed that prior to having been cut by the team, she was sexually assaulted by the coach, a teacher/coach by the name of Daren Steele. Daren was in his mid-thirties, married, and taught science courses. He hailed from California and had been employed at Las Cruces High School for six years.

According to Daren's accuser, she, at his request, had stayed after practice late one afternoon so that he could give her some extra pointers. While in an equipment shed, he had her disrobe and then fondled her. Apparently, this happened several more times over the next week, and when she refused the last time, she was cut from the team.

When Daren was confronted by the school authorities and later by the police, he categorically denied the accusations. He was extremely upset because word got out, and said he was already crucified in the press and thus in public opinion. He agreed to take a polygraph and in the interim was put on administrative leave. Unfortunately for Daren, the polygraph results were deemed deceptive, and Morrey filed felony sexual assault charges.

Shortly after Daren bonded out, his wife left him, taking their two small children with her. The newspaper had not been kind to him, and his friends and associates soon distanced themselves from him. With no family, friends, or job, Daren fell into a deep depression, resulting in his taking his own life.

Within weeks, Daren's accuser was in the district attorney's office claiming that the whole incident was a hoax. She made up the whole story! Her closest friend who made the track team conspired with her, thinking it would result in termination of the coach and reinstatement of the accuser. They hadn't counted on anything like this. Things had gotten out of hand. She was sorry.

The same polygrapher responsible for Daren's polygraph administered one to Daren's accuser. The polygrapher found no deception. The accuser passed the polygraph with flying colors. The accuser, despite Daren's polygraph results, had made up the whole story. Daren was completely exonerated, albeit much too late.

When Morrey met with the polygrapher, who was a full-time employee of the Las Cruces Police Department, he asked how it was possible Daren flunked the polygraph when he was telling the truth. The polygrapher stated that sometimes it's the phraseology of the questions, but most often it is because the accusations are so inherently offensive and piercing, especially to someone like Daren, where everything was riding on the results, that the internal emotional trauma caused a reaction that simulated a deception.

"Interpretation is not always precise," he admitted, "and if the polygrapher is convinced one way or the other, that could also skew the results." He wasn't sure what the cause was here and added, "That's why polygraph results are not scientifically recognized."

The polygrapher then had a piercing question for Morrey: "Why didn't you polygraph the accuser to begin with?"

Morrey put it back on the polygrapher's shoulders. "Because according to your results, Daren had failed the polygraph!"

Despite his answer, Morrey was not convinced of the rationale. Why hadn't he polygraphed the victim before filing charges? That was something he specifically would be asking himself time and time again as he watched his own children become adults and have children of their own. He would often wonder what became of the wife and the children of the teacher/coach who had been wrongfully accused of and charged with sexual assault. Even now he was wondering if Daren's ex-wife and children knew that the accused sexual predator was not a predator at all but the victim of a sick and pitiful hoax. And worst of all, Morrey had been a part of it. It would be bad enough living with the memory that your daddy had been charged with a serious crime, but not knowing that your daddy was innocent of that crime would be far worse—maybe life-altering. The collateral effect at the time had not been considered.

• • •

It was the district attorney's duty to seek justice, not obtain convictions. Had he been focusing on the wrong things? Using his talent and skills to seek justice was one thing, but to use one's talent and skills to seek a victory was something that was not supposed to be in the equation. An overzealous prosecutor could obtain a conviction of an innocent defendant, but that would be a travesty of justice. He had proven that just by filing criminal charges on an innocent man can have the same disastrous consequences as convicting an innocent man. Morrey wondered if maybe he had been guilty of both.

• • •

Morrey then remembered the case of the pharmacist's son, Travis, who worked for his father after school and at graduation time stole a handful of psychedelic drugs from the pharmacy and surreptitiously dumped them in the punch bowl at the senior prom. One of the unwitting samplers was Tanya, the daughter of a local preacher. An ambulance was called when she went into convulsions. Years later she was still being treated for her intermittent hallucinations.

Morrey was criticized for charging Travis, who had just days before the incident turned eighteen, with a felony, specifically, inducing consumption of controlled substances by fraudulent means. When Morrey refused to lower the charges, there was even more public outrage. And seeking and obtaining a prison sentence caused even the school authorities to clamor.

The reason Morrey was agonizing over the decision now, and he had found himself revisiting it many times in the past, was that shortly after Travis' prison admittance, the little rich kid who spiked the school punch bowl was the target of a rebellious group in the exercise pen, and their rough tactics resulted in Travis's death. Travis was eighteen and a half years old at the time. His parents blamed Morrey for their son's death, and family members still make hateful comments to Morrey when they pass him on the street. Needless to say, the Dexter family was compelled to find another pharmacy to frequent.

• • •

Oscar and Ada Vercelli were in their late fifties and lived in a trailer park on the outskirts of Las Cruces. It was not uncommon for Ada to call the sheriff's office after Oscar returned home from one of his Saturday night binges with the boys and have her husband arrested claiming domestic violence. Ada would have Sunday morning remorse, and demanding that charges be dropped, rescue Oscar from the county slammer.

After receiving a telephone call from the neighbor at 2:30 a.m. on that cold, wintery Sunday morning, the sheriff's deputies arrived at the Vercelli trailer to find a crumpled Ada unconscious on the floor. With a broken nose and two black eyes, Ada had proven to be no match for her drunken husband.

Ada was taken to the Mercy Hospital ER; Oscar was taken to the Paraiso County jail. He was arrested and charged with felony assault and domestic violence. This time, Ada didn't immediately run down and bond out the wife beater. Three days later, however, she appeared in

Morrey's office stating she wanted charges dropped and her husband released. To convince Morrey to drop the charges, Ada had claimed she made up the story and that her injuries had been caused not by Oscar but by her having fallen down the basement steps while carrying a load of laundry.

Speaking with the Department of Human Services, it was agreed that if Oscar went to rehab, charges would be dropped. Oscar complied, and he was placed on an out-patient treatment plan. With an unwilling victim and no other eyewitnesses, the authorities' hands were pretty much tied.

Agreeing not to pursue criminal prosecution was tantamount to a death sentence for Ada, because shortly after Oscar returned home, a paper boy called 911 reporting that Ada's body was lying at the base of her front steps. When the deputy sheriffs arrived, Ada could not be revived. She would not be calling 911 again or anyone else, for that matter. Oscar, who was found inside the trailer sleeping off his latest stupor, had silenced Ada forever.

The very people who had taken an oath to protect their constituents, that is, the DA, the sheriff, and the caseworker, were asleep at the switch. They had woefully failed to protect Ada despite the numerous warnings and cries for help and myriad opportunities. They were enablers.

They enabled Oscar to finish the job he had started. In DA parlance, they were complicitors.

• • •

Morrey also thought of a similar case that had occurred the previous summer when the fifteen-year-old daughter of a migrant worker had reported to authorities that her parents had been physically abusing her. She was taken to a physician, and examination disclosed multiple bruises on the upper thighs and the buttocks. When the Department of Human Services interviewed her parents, it was determined that she had been having a sexual relationship with the sixteen-year-old son of another migrant worker and that both sets of parents had forbidden the two to see each other. When caught disobeying their parents' orders, both received corporal punishment and were confined to their respective parents' quarters. The fifteen-year-old girl broke free and contacted authorities.

When the girl met with Toby and Morrey, she confirmed the story. After a meeting with both families, the investigating officers, the caseworker, and the physician, it was determined that the injuries had not been life-threatening and that the girl's parents in the future would confer with the county psychologist about less drastic alternatives of discipline. The two young people had agreed not to see each other again, and everything appeared copasetic.

In less than a week, the body of the girl was lying on a cold steel slab at the morgue. Apparently, her father had caught his daughter and the young man in a compromising position. He was not very understanding, and being a big man, administered a brand of heavy-handed discipline that resulted in the hospitalization of the young man and the death of his daughter.

Another wasted life—one that could have been spared if only the authorities had done their job. The outcome was predictable, and yet those in charge turned a blind eye toward the situation. By their irresponsibility, they sealed the fate of this young girl. Morrey wondered how many other deaths it would take before the authorities got religion in both the traditional and nontraditional sense.

If someone had told Morrey when he was first elected that he would have power over life and death, he wouldn't have believed it. Nearly completing his twelfth year as district attorney and seeing his life as a prosecutor flash before him, he no longer was a doubting Thomas. Perhaps if he had known, he would have been frightened away and embarked on a less precarious career—at least one that wouldn't be haunting him the rest of his life.

CHAPTER 15

Destiny Calls

Attending a legal seminar in Denver and while visiting at break with the attorney who had been sitting next to him, Morrey learned that the attorney's grandfather had been a district attorney in western Colorado. His grandfather, who had been active in student affairs at Princeton University, told him about butting heads with the then-president of Princeton over a fraternity issue. He said as a result of the feud, the two became fast friends.

His grandfather then went on to relate that the president of Princeton encouraged him to become a lawyer and ultimately a district attorney. The president said he was impressed by the grandfather's dedication and determination in fighting for something he strongly believed in. He then went on to tell the grandfather something that was apparent only after it was revealed: "The two most powerful positions in the United States are the district attorneys in their respective districts and the president of the United States." The name of the then-president of Princeton? Woodrow Wilson, who later became the twenty-eighth president of the United States.

• • •

The last order of business for Morrey as district attorney was to accept the bronze plaque memorializing his "Outstanding Contribution to Professional Prosecution" as a three-term district attorney for the district. Presenting the award at Morrey's retirement was Assistant District Attorney Kimbal L. Medina, Terrence R. Brockerton's replacement when the latter was appointed county judge. Kimbal would be sworn in as Morrey's replacement the following Tuesday, the first Tuesday of January. Officially, that was Morrey's last day as district attorney and Kimbal's first day as the newly elected district attorney.

When the crowd clamored for a speech, Morrey, haltingly at first and still clutching the plaque, began, "It's easy to understand why our Creator didn't give us as standard equipment the ability to see into the future. It might dissuade some of us from venturing out, knowing what awaited us. At least there's hope and expectation when venturing into the unknown. I would want to relive my twelve years as district attorney only if I could alter the course and do some things differently. Otherwise, I would not want to go back.

"From time to time as a district attorney, I

found myself in deep, murky waters, some where I couldn't touch bottom and was way over my head. In my journey as district attorney, I found myself caught in some storms and sailed in some pretty turbulent seas, but the good Lord always navigated me through. For the most part, however, our ship sailed on relatively calm oceans thanks to many who are here tonight and others who unfortunately were unable to attend.

"I was taught at a young age by my father, who I know is here in spirit, that once you lose your own self-respect, you've lost everything. I've taken that to heart all my life and especially my life as a prosecutor. There are tough calls to be made, and as you know all too well, not all of them are popular. Prosecutorial discretion, when used improperly, can have disastrous consequences. I only hope, when the final tally is posted, that I will be found not to have abused my prosecutorial discretion. It's not only the district attorney who must live or die by the sword, but all those who are affected by the district attorney's decisions.

"My approval rating over the years was like watching an electrocardiogram tracing an irregular heartbeat. It fluctuated depending on who was being prosecuted and who was being convicted. The public I found to be fickle and unpredictable.

As one of our state legislators recently told me, 'You can determine public sentiment by what direction the wind blows.' In November, my approval rating was over ninety percent. That's the highest it's ever been and maybe that's because I announced I would not be running for reelection. However, I think it was because of my staff and the other agencies in our district's criminal justice system that made me look good. I thank all of you for making me look good. Working with you has been an honor, something I shall always cherish.

"As I conclude this chapter in my life, whatever successes I might have enjoyed were because somebody up there was always looking out for me. Even though I let my Lord down from time to time, he never let me down. Thank you, God—Father, Son, and Holy Spirit. If the good Lord had not put my parents in my life, I wouldn't be standing here today. My mother and father taught me love of God, country, family, and neighbor. They also taught me values and respect for the law. My failings were not because of them. To Sergio, my surrogate father, who introduced me to and fostered my knowledge of the criminal law, I can't thank enough. To Toby, my boyhood friend and devoted investigator, I'm hoping to take you to the attorney general's office with me.

To my family, who has stood by me through thick and thin, I hope I'm as important to you as you are to me. All of you come stand by me and take this curtain call with me.

"While you are coming forward, I want to say Monique, the girls, and I will be maintaining our principal residence here in Las Cruces. In fact, until the school year is concluded, Monique and the girls will remain in Las Cruces. Thereafter they will join me in Denver.

"I will always hold you deep within my heart and am grateful to God for having placed you in my life."

Morrey knew there was no turning back. Destiny was beckoning.

• • •

It was the second Tuesday in January, and Morrey was sworn in as the new Colorado attorney general. He had been battle-ready at the district level, and as the state's chief law enforcement officer, he now had to be battle-ready at the state level. Crystal's prophecy had been fulfilled; he had defeated the incumbent, and he was moving into a new, challenging season—one that would change his life forever.

Starting a new job and moving to Denver without Monique and his daughters was not an ideal arrangement, but it would have to do until his daughters finished the school year. The small, drab studio apartment on Capitol Hill in a drab building in a drab neighborhood would have to do until he found more suitable quarters. At least the price was right, and he was within walking distance of his office. Toby, whom he had hired as chief investigator, had the apartment next door.

Soon, both Morrey and Toby found larger apartments in a better part of town. Even though the attorney general no longer had an office in the state capitol building, he still had an official parking space. It was next to the governor's.

• • •

It was Easter Monday, an almost summer-like day, and the time was close to 6:00 p.m. Both Morrey and Governor Wellington Prescott arrived at their vehicles parked in their officially assigned spaces at about the same time. The governor came around the front of the vehicle to where Morrey was standing, and the two shook hands and exchanged greetings. They had stood there but a few moments before shots rang out from across the street. *Bang! Bang! Bang! Bang! Bang!*

It was obvious the target was Governor Prescott, a dignified statesman in his late fifties. His undoing was trying to hang onto his car door handle to keep from falling. He was hit four times, the last bullet penetrating his left temple. The first three shots were not fatal. Morrey, in an attempt to find cover in the front of his vehicle, was struck by a fifth shot—a ricocheting bullet that lodged in the lumbar region of his spine.

Both were transported by ambulance to the closest hospital. Governor Prescott was pronounced dead upon arrival. Morrey couldn't move his lower extremities and feared the worst. He could hear the footsteps outside his door and recognized the voice of Dr. Sherwood talking to a nurse. He could feel his heart beat hasten as Dr. Sherwood entered his hospital room.

"How's my favorite patient?" Dr. Sherwood asked in a cheerful voice.

"I'll bet you call all your patients your favorite," Morrey replied.

"Only my most favorite ones. How are you feeling today?"

"I still don't have any feeling in my lower extremities. Everything is numb, as if my limbs are asleep. I can't seem to move them at all."

Dr. Sherwood pulled the covers down to the foot of the bed and carefully examined Morrey from the upper pelvis down. He would ask if Morrey had feeling as he navigated his way to the bottom of

Morrey's feet. Each time Morrey would indicate that he had none.

Morrey could stand the suspense no longer and blurted out, "I'm paralyzed from the waist down, aren't I?"

"The good news is that the ricocheting bullet lost some of its velocity when it struck the car's metal before striking you, or otherwise it would have been fatal. The bad news is that the bullet has rendered you a paraplegic. I'm sorry I have to tell you that."

Morrey wondered how Dr. Sherwood could be so blunt and matter-of-fact. Dr. Sherwood had warned him of the medical fears and had tried to prepare him for this moment. However, there had been that glimmer of hope which now had dissipated into a confrontation with reality. He now knew he would never walk again.

Morrey waited until after Dr. Sherwood left the room before the torrent of tears and anguish manifested themselves. Instead of despair and surrender, he soon felt an inexplicable peace within. After all, he was still alive, and what he had been making a living with, his brain, was still intact. He could still enjoy his family and friends. There were just parts of his body that he could no longer use. He had always been resilient and could make adjustments. Since life gave him lemons, he would make the best of it and make lemonade. He may have been forced to bend, but he was not broken.

• • •

As a district attorney, Morrey had received numerous death threats, none of which had been disclosed to Monique or the girls. When he had conducted grand jury investigations, he was told by a man who was being investigated for homicide in an insurance fraud case in which the man "accidentally" shot and killed his business partner while hunting elk that *if* he were a vindictive man, which he said he *wasn't*, he would come looking for Morrey's daughters. He knew what they looked like, their ages, the school they went to, and where and what times they boarded the school bus and returned home.

On another occasion, when Morrey was jogging down a deserted county country road after work one evening, he was introduced to the ping of a slug as it passed overhead. This was during the meth fiasco. He would hear that same sound several more times during his third term in office. The most death threats he had received in the shortest period of time was during Bruce Spangberg's first criminal prosecution. After the first death threats, traces were put on the calls. All came from a payphone near Dr. Spangberg's dental office. Even though some of the phone calls were tape recorded and fingerprints lifted, the mystery still remained as to the identity of the caller.

Morrey had been Colorado attorney general for only ninety days. It was apparent that he had not made any enemies, or at least none who would resort to such drastic measures. Governor Prescott, on the other hand, was starting his second term, and ever since his election to public office, first as an attorney general and then as governor, had been vocal in the crackdown on organized crime and environmental violations. He had targeted some large business enterprises that purportedly had been illegally disposing of hazardous waste in the sewers of Denver and outlying areas.

Many rumors spread, and the governor's death was subjected to outlandish speculation. There was talk that the governor had been having an affair with an aide and that her irate husband took matters into his own hands. There was also talk that the governor had not delivered on a promise of a gubernatorial pardon where the felon's relatives had paid the exacted consideration. Regardless, the governor did not deserve to die, and the detractors were libeling the dead. That was criminal libel.

• • •

Morrey was disturbed by the conflict within. He stubbornly fought the psychological and physiological effects of his paralysis. It was more difficult to adapt than he had anticipated. He was now dependent on others even for the mundane. He didn't want to be a burden on Monique and his staff, but he knew he was and would always be. But then again, if *they* didn't complain then why should he?

Morrey was becoming adept with the operation of his wheelchair, and the wheels were soon becoming his legs. He was not deterred in his mobility or his resolve by being confined to his four-wheeler, as he referred to it. He was learning to be resourceful and find ways to compensate for his physical infirmity. He was becoming mentally tough and more determined than ever to carry out the details of his office as the chief law enforcement officer of the state. His mettle was being tested, and he found he was up to the challenge.

With Sergio's help, Monique found a newly constructed one-level home in the Denver suburbs. Since most of the new construction in the surrounding area was multi-level, the Dexters felt fortunate. With the addition of a ramp, both front and back, Morrey was able to enter and exit with ease. With school having come to a close for the year, the family was reunited. Some things would be different, but where it really counted, they would be the same or better.

The personal mail had piled up on Morrey's desk while he was on medical leave. Morrey, while sorting through the mail, found a letter that had arrived on the day he had been shot. It was from Crystal, and it had been postmarked several weeks before. It apparently had been misdirected and sat in someone's delay pile for quite some time. It read:

> *Dear Morrey:*
> *I hesitate to write this letter but feel compelled.*
>
> *I had a psychic impression last night that a small white van following a large tank truck with lettering on the side had slowed down long enough to allow the passenger in the front and the one in the back to fire five shots.*
>
> *I watched as both you and a distinguished gray-haired gentleman fell to the ground. There weren't too many cars in the parking lot next to what I presume was your capitol building, so I assume it was at day's end.*
>
> *I'm not sure whether I observed something that happened in the past or something yet to come.*

I hope it is the latter so that it can be averted.
The only lettering I could make out on the
dingy tank truck was "QUIN."

As ever — Crystal.

The investigation revealed that three of the slugs that hit the governor were fired from the same weapon. Both the fourth slug that struck the governor and the fifth one that struck Morrey were fired from a second weapon. Witnesses in the apartment building across the street after hearing what sounded like shots looked out their windows in time to see an old tank truck amble around the corner followed by a white van, with both disappearing down the alley on the far side of the apartment building. They had taken no particular note, thinking that the noise they heard was due to the backfiring of the larger truck.

Morrey immediately summoned Toby. Toby read Crystal's letter and forthwith grabbed the Denver telephone directory. When Toby looked up waste disposal, the name Quinton Disposal Service, Inc., caught his eye. Between Crystal and Toby, the shooting of the governor and the attorney general would soon be solved and the perpetrators ultimately brought to justice.

• • •

Life became a little more problematic for Morrey, and he became very cynical. Thinking for a long time that he had been too tough on the criminal element, he was now beginning to feel he had not been tough enough. When he discovered that the perpetrators of the drive-by shooting had extensive criminal records, he knew the prosecutors, judges, probation officers, correction officers, and parole board connected with their cases were undoubtedly guilty of dereliction of duty.

Giving offenders second, third, fourth, and maybe even more chances made the criminal justice agencies enablers and complicitors and the criminal justice system a mockery. In his eyes, they aided, abetted, assisted, and encouraged recidivism. Morrey admitted *they* included *him*. They were as bad as the criminals themselves—maybe even worse. At least criminals had perceived excuses; the so-called criminal justice experts had none.

Compassion was just another word for profound passiveness, gullibility, and lassitude. Even in the business world, the supervisor is held responsible for the acts of his or her subordinates. So, why not in the world where consequences can be more disastrous and maybe even fatal?

Morrey never felt the innocent should suffer while the guilty reaped the benefits. In a symbiotic relationship where the parasite enjoys a fruitful existence at the expense of its host, the parasite normally dies when the host dies. *Not true in our criminal justice system,* he thought. When the host dies, society just provides the parasite with another host. To treat the perpetrator as inhumane as the perpetrator treated the victim is deemed to be cruel and unusual punishment. There are severe penalties for that. That's not something society would or should tolerate. Right? Morrey remembered receiving the file on a case he had inherited when he first became district attorney for a fifth-grade teacher, where the teacher had a boy stand in the corner for setting fire to the hair of the girl who sat in front of him. The father was upset because the teacher embarrassed his son in front of the class and wanted the teacher fired. When the principal and the school board refused, he tried to get Morrey's predecessor to file criminal charges. The father ultimately sued the school district, and the school district's insurance carrier settled out of court. The young boy became a hero because of his so-called courageous stand against the "oppression" of school authority. The young boy's name, interestingly enough, was Bruce Spangberg. His father's name was Dr. Sydney

Spangberg. No surprise there! *More often than not*, Morrey surmised, *little criminals grow up to be big criminals.*

• • •

While Morrey had been recovering in the hospital, he had a lot of time to think. He knew that all but a small number who were sent to prison were returned to society. The criminal justice system was designed ostensibly first to punish the wrongdoer; secondly, to serve as a deterrent not only to the wrongdoer but to others who might have a propensity or proclivity to do the same; thirdly, to insulate society from a continuation of criminal conduct from the offender; and lastly, to rehabilitate the offender so that upon release he or she would not reoffend. *Release from incarceration*, he thought, *should only be after the offender was determined not to be a risk to society.* Morrey felt the good of society governed over the good of the individual. However, Morrey recognized that both society and the individual suffered while the individual was incarcerated. The dilemma was how to recycle the offender so as to make him or her productive to himself or herself and thereby be productive to society. By trying to balance countervailing rights and equities and to think outside the square, Morrey would, however, be judged favorably by history.

CHAPTER 16

Crossing Over

When Morrey returned to Las Cruces, he was received with a hero's welcome. Local boy had made good! The headlines in the *Las Cruces Gazette* read **FAVORITE SON RETURNS**. Even the recently completed city auditorium carried his name.

At the dedication, the crowd cheered and applauded as he was introduced. Morrey knew he wasn't as profound as the crowd indicated by their enthusiastic reaction to everything he said. He hadn't been that nervous since exchanging vows with Monique. The outpouring of love from the well-wishers made him feel like a rock star. Morrey was back to his point of beginning!

• • •

At age forty-seven, Morrey was still in the prime of his life. He had not yet turned all the windmills right-side up. He still had a vision and a desire to continue seeking justice. He opened an office in a main street building held in the Santana Trust. The office was on the ground floor and not far from the courthouse.

In anticipation of Morrey's return and Julia's

graduation from law school and admission to the Colorado Bar, a large suite containing two spacious oak-paneled and scenery-friendly executive offices were at the ready. Morrey's old private library was updated and the new library was already the most extensive on this side of Denver. There was also an extra office for future expansion.

Jenny Saunders had resigned her position with a rival law firm and once again would be Morrey's head secretary. Monique was fitted with an office in the suite and became the firm's bookkeeper. There she would wear another hat, that of a writer. Several of her short stories had been published in various periodicals, and she was already working on her third novel, *The Last Cross Standing*.

• • •

It was not long before Julia graduated from law school and was admitted to the practice of law. It was with great pride that Morrey changed the name of the firm to *Dexter & Dexter, Attorneys at Law*. The time had gone by quickly, and even though Morrey said he wouldn't, he was soon embroiled in the defense of those charged with allegedly having committed crimes. Of course, he and Julia would contend that they were representing only the *unjustly* accused.

When asked how it felt to switch to the other side, Morrey's canned response was, "I haven't switched. I'm still on the same side—the side of justice." He not only said it; he believed it.

CHAPTER 17

Defending the Innocent

Before long, Morrey found himself engaged in a number of high profile criminal cases and was obtaining acquittals that were receiving widespread attention. He was now a highly sought-after *defense attorney*. Instead of prosecuting public officials, he was now successfully representing them and many of the notorious. None received more attention than the representation of Holly Lundi, a young mother charged in the death of her eight month-old daughter, Michelle, or "Missy," as she was called.

Holly was the twenty-three-year-old daughter of the Santanas' neighbors, Lloyd and Lydia Davies. Her ancestors were longtime residents of Las Cruces. When Holly returned from Pepperdine with a bachelor of science degree in journalism, she was hired on at the *Las Cruces Gazette* as a reporter. Holly's writing skills earned her the prestigious position of covering the court beat. She appeared to relish her assignment and had a weekly column profiling locals who were making a difference in the community. Holly's good looks caught the attention of the editor's son, Ryan

Lundi, who was twelve years Holly's senior. They began dating and soon married.

Ryan and Holly were a perfect match. Ryan was being groomed to take over as editor of the newspaper, and his journalistic talents and business acumen already overshadowed that of his father.

Holly and Ryan with Missy were inseparable and had a true Camelot existence. Both came from wealth and started married life with a newly constructed, imposing ranch-style stone home on eighty acres near Holly's parents. Both drove late-model automobiles. With the birth of Missy, Holly was assigned the white Cadillac SUV.

In her last trimester of her pregnancy, Holly had cut her hours at the *Gazette*, and upon the birth of little Missy, Holly's journalistic aspirations were temporarily placed on hold.

• • •

On that hot, humid Friday marking the start of the Fourth of July weekend, the Paraiso County sheriff 's office received a frantic telephone call reporting a missing child. The caller asked to speak to Sergio.

"Sergio, this is Holly Lundi." Between sobs, Holly related that she was calling on her cellphone and was at the Twin Pines Shopping Center and had just returned to her SUV with groceries to find her daughter missing. Missy was sleeping soundly after a fitful night, and Holly didn't want to disturb her. Foolishly, she had left Missy in the car with the windows rolled up and hadn't locked the doors. She was gone longer that she had planned, and finding Missy missing, had been searching high and low for her. She had left Missy strapped in the car seat and knew Missy was incapable of freeing herself, let alone exiting the vehicle.

Sergio had known Holly since her birth. The families had been friends for literally generations. Even though it was a matter for the Las Cruces Police Department, Sergio grabbed a deputy and headed for the Twin Pines Shopping Center. Holly was sitting in her vehicle as Sergio had instructed when he and Deputy Britt Korland arrived. She was obviously distraught but became hysterical upon seeing Sergio. He tried to comfort her while Britt started the search. Soon, Las Cruces police officers were dispatched, and employees and customers inside of the shopping center businesses were detained and interviewed concerning Missy's whereabouts. Ryan was called and he and his father aided in the search.

Word spread like wildfire about Missy's disappearance. Law enforcement officers and search and rescue units from around the area were soon involved in the search. Simultaneously, the press from near and far descended on Las Cruces. Holly was whisked away to seclusion but not before making statements that later would be reported. Within short order, Holly, Ryan, and members of their respective families made public pleas with the aid of the electronic media, begging for the return or information leading to the return of little Missy.

Precious hours and then days turned up no sign of Missy. Despite the persistent pleas and outpouring of support for the family, all leads resulted in dead-ends. At wits' end, the family sought the aid of the FBI. Still, no clues regarding Missy's disappearance.

• • •

Holly's father stood at his window looking out when he noticed something unusual at his daughter's home. In the backyard, he saw smoke. *It would be unusual to burn with the fire ban still in effect*, he thought. He had seen his daughter drive off earlier and decided that maybe he should investigate. He discovered upon examining the smoldering coals what appeared to be charred fragments of a baby blanket. He picked up a nearby shovel and upon probing the freshly turned soil found something of which only nightmares were made.

Lloyd called Sergio, and within less than an hour, Missy was no longer considered a missing child or the victim of a kidnapping. The nightmare for the family, however, was just beginning. After interviewing Holly, the investigation was now one involving a possible criminal homicide.

• • •

Upon discovery of her daughter's body, Holly admitted the disappearance/kidnap was a hoax—a cover-up. She said the story about going to the shopping center, leaving the sleeping child in the car, and shopping too long was all true. The rest for the most part was false. When she arrived at the car and found that Missy was not breathing, she immediately panicked. She felt guilty about leaving Missy alone in the car on that exceedingly hot day with the windows rolled tight. She said that the night before, Missy had a fever, and she was up with Missy literally the whole night trying to comfort and care for her. Leaving her in the car, she thought, was in Missy's best interest. In retrospect, she would not have done so. Not thinking straight and fearful of what her husband and their families would say and do, she embarked on the cover-up.

She said she drove home and deposited Missy still wrapped in a blanket in the garden at the rear of their home. She then piled a stack of small dead tree limbs and dry weeds on top of Missy's makeshift grave as a camouflage. She then immediately returned to the shopping center and called Sergio, staging a missing child/kidnap. She vehemently denied having killed her daughter. She loved her much too much to do something like that. She stated it was only much later that she set the pile ablaze.

• • •

During the autopsy and examination by the county corner and a forensic pathologist, it was determined that because some soot was discovered in Missy's windpipe, Missy must have been alive at the time she was burned. The case was turned over to the district attorney's office. Irving Eagleton, the current district attorney, had a difficult charging decision to make. Since he didn't think Holly had the intent to terminate Missy's life, and in all likelihood didn't knowingly cause her death, he opted for manslaughter. Manslaughter made it a felony to recklessly cause another's death, and that was the least with which Eagleton thought Holly should be charged. He also charged felony child abuse because Holly had unreasonably placed Missy in a situation which posed a threat of injury to the life and health of Missy, resulting in her death, and of course, tampering with evidence, also a felony. In addition to the felonies, Holly was charged with the following misdemeanors: false reporting, concealment of a death, and abuse of a corpse.

The lives of the Lundis and the Davies had been turned upside down as a result of Missy's death and the charges against Holly. Upon her arrest and release on bail, Holly literally went into seclusion. She didn't want to see or talk to anyone. When she was brought into Morrey's office, she came in reluctantly. As far as she was concerned, she deserved the death penalty and that what she had done was indefensible and unforgivable.

The $100,000 retainer that Morrey received was the largest that he would ever receive. He would bill against that amount and return the remainder. That was the amount the Lundis and the Davies brought to his office and insisted he take. They wanted the best for Holly and would pay whatever it took to prove her innocence. That would also be the first and only involvement in an infanticide defense during Morrey's legal career.

The first thing Morrey did was to hire a pathologist of his own. Dr. Virgil Vaughn, in examining the corpse, determined that there was only a speck of soot or carbon particles in Missy's windpipe which could just as likely have ended up there post-mortem or maybe even inadvertently induced while the autopsy was being performed by the county corner and the state's forensic pathologist. When Holly was advised of Dr. Vaughn's findings, she sobbed now knowing for certain that Missy was not alive when she was burned.

• • •

Julia was still a partner in the law firm of Dexter & Dexter. However, upon her marriage to Bray Carlton, a young attorney who had set up practice in Las Cruces the year before Julia graduated from law school, Bray became a partner in the firm. The firm was now known as *Dexter, Dexter-Carlton & Carlton*. Julia was twenty-seven and was now pregnant with the couple's first child. She had evolved into a very competent defense lawyer, "a chip off the old block," Morrey would brag. She would be co-counsel in the infanticide defense.

Morrey and Julia would file the usual array of defense motions only to have them for the most part denied. Shay Bisben was now the chief judge and assigned himself to the case. Morrey had tried several major cases before Judge Bisben since Morrey's return and found him to be extremely competent. Not too many of his decisions would be reversed. *To be competent, fair, and unassuming, all at the same time, was a rare quality for the judiciary these days, Morrey thought.*

Morrey found it a rare privilege to have his daughter as a law partner. It was something he had dreamt of and hoped for but never expected. She had some extraordinary insight into the minds of most of the clients the firm defended, particularly in this one. Perhaps it was because of her own pregnancy, but Julia offered a perspective that even escaped Morrey.

Julia in interviewing Holly detected that Holly was suffering from postpartum depression. She asked Holly about the possibility, and Holly related that indeed she had sought counseling after Missy's birth because of periods of deep depression. She was still seeing a psychologist, though only on a sporadic basis. Julia then obtained a medical release form from Holly and spoke with the psychologist, Dr. Kidman Yhlem. Dr. Yhlem confirmed that Holly was her patient and that she had prescribed antidepressants shortly after Missy's birth. Holly, however, seemed to have adjusted and responded remarkably well, and after the first six months following Missy's birth, Holly had been taken off the medication.

Morrey was in a quandary. If Holly hadn't deliberately caused Missy's death, then temporary insanity would be like saying Holly didn't do it, *but if she did,* she was insane at the time. Her state of mind when she made unwise decisions such as leaving the child alone in an oven of a car on a hot day or opting for a cover-up might be relevant. However, Holly's mind was operating effectively enough at the time to conjure up a fairly elaborate scheme to keep secret her blunders. On the other hand, to avoid recrimination from the man she loved and spare him and Missy's grandparents the pain, fabrication could be a viable alternative even for the most righteous among us.

Early in his career, Morrey had scoffed at the idea that a father would take his daughter off insulin and opt instead for a natural health cure. In fact, he had prosecuted, albeit unsuccessfully, the father for endangering the life of his child. Now he was asking the world to believe that a mother would leave her baby cooped up in a hot car on a hot day, and feeling responsible for the baby's death, would burn the corpse, even though she was not criminally culpable. *That was kind of a double standard, wasn't it?* Morrey asked himself. Child endangerment in one case and not in another? A parent's reaction in one ill-advised, but totally explainable and understandable in the other? Yet he believed wholeheartedly in Holly's cause and was determined to obtain her complete vindication. The only thing Holly was guilty of was poor judgment.

Isn't that what the parents claimed lo those many years ago when they substituted a health potion for insulin resulting in their daughter's death?

• • •

It was autumn and the leaves, which had turned their patented shades of rose and gold, were falling like snow. Chill was in the air, and the locals knew winter was lurking not far behind. Julia was pushing her father at a rather brisk pace up the ramp and into the all-familiar courthouse. The basket carrying the books and files on the back of the wheelchair and Julia's protruding tummy made the trek somewhat awkward. It was the first day of trial in the infanticide prosecution of *People v. Lundi.*

In a courtroom resembling a Hollywood set for a Clarence Darrow trial scene sat the jury panel from which the jurors would be selected to pass judgment on one of their own. Morrey was wheeled to defense counsel's table to arrange the trial paraphernalia in the easily retrievable stacks reminiscent of his other trials while Julia went into the hall to await Holly's arrival. Within short order, with her arm through Julia's, Holly was led to her seat positioned between Morrey and Julia.

Irving Eagleton, together with his chief trial deputy and chief investigator, arrived with armloads of books, files, documents, and miscellaneous and sundry prosecutorial amenities. Morrey thought for a moment they had also brought their lunch. Kiddingly, Morrey asked Irving how they were fixed for socks. Their cajoling was akin to the high fives between opposing players after the coin toss. Trial was like a sporting event in other ways. They would be granting each other no quarter until the contest was complete, and even then, they might have to be coerced into shaking hands.

The bailiff announced the entrance of the presiding judge, the Honorable Shay Bisben. Judge Bisben plopped down in his high-backed leather chair and donned his spectacles. Motioning for everyone else to be seated, he announced the court was in session. Peering over the top of his spectacles, he nodded to the clerk for her to begin the jury selection process in the case of *People v. Lundi.*

Morrey had asked Ryan and the respective families to absent themselves from all phases of the trial, including jury selection. Since they or some of them might be called as witnesses, under the sequestration rule they would be barred from attending most of the trial anyway. Judge Bisben had ordered that the rule be followed at *all* stages. That way, they would not be conforming their testimony when they testified to what they heard in the courtroom. It would not be a very uplifting experience for the family anyway and would only enhance their level of anxiety. Also, Morrey wanted to respect Holly's wishes in that regard. She preferred that family and friends stay away—at least for now.

It was difficult to gauge public sentiment in this case since the newspaper was owned by the Lundis, and little appeared therein after the investigation centered on Holly. No letters to the editor were printed after that date. What news that did appear was fair and accurate. Therefore, it was unlikely that the prospective jurors had been tainted by any pretrial publicity.

In profiling the ideal juror to sit in judgment of Holly, Morrey and Julia were undecided. Initially at least, Morrey thought women, particularly older women, would be more judgmental. Julia thought they would be more understanding, especially those who were mothers. Morrey thought young men would be swayed by Holly's charm; Julia thought just the opposite. She thought those who had been spurned by a Holly might seek vengeance, whereas a fatherly type might have more empathy. Both thought those with sisters and/or daughters might be more sympathetic regardless of gender.

Ultimately, both agreed the married versus the unmarried might be preferable.

Morrey had been successful in the past by following his gut feeling. Whether male or female, young or old, single or married, divorced or separated, old-time residents or newbies, management or labor, skilled or unskilled, religious or nonbelievers, liberal or conservative, schooled or unschooled, rich or poor, or skin color, if you have a queasy feeling about keeping that person, get rid of him or her. That was his mantra. In other words, when in doubt, press the ejection button if you can and strike the questionable juror. Otherwise, the juror's selection might come back to haunt you.

The one good thing the defense had going for them was that in order to convict, the verdict had to be unanimous. All they needed was one holdout to hang the jury. At least a hung or undecided jury was better than a conviction. The worst that could happen was that they just started over.

In the last analysis, selecting the jury was really the luck of the draw. It was like the lottery or playing bingo. Who wins and who loses depends on the name or number drawn. If you use up all your allotted challenges and can't challenge for cause, you may end up with a more unfavorable juror than the one that you had just replaced.

Unfortunately, that is exactly what happened in Holly's case. They hoped that was not a bad omen—at least not for the defense.

The jury, they would have to live with. It was not great nor was it deplorable. It was somewhere in between, which meant it would probably be fair not just to one side or the other, but both sides.

• • •

In his opening statement, Eagleton outlined the evidence the prosecution would present. He said: "The evidence will show that the accused left her eight-month-old child strapped in a car seat in the family's unattended vehicle while she went inside a grocery store to shop. With the temperatures soaring into the nineties, she closed all the windows but left the doors unlocked. After spending more than the intended time in the store, by her own admission, she emerged with her groceries to find her child not breathing—at least according to her assessment."

Shuffling through his notes, Eagleton continued by saying: "The accused told authorities she thought her child was dead. Terrified of breaking the horrific news to the baby's father and relatives, she said she devised a scheme to make it look like a kidnapping. She said she then drove to the family home and hid the baby in her backyard. Thereafter, she hastened back to the store parking lot and called the sheriff 's office to report the child missing."

In telling the jury the evidence would establish Holly's guilt beyond a reasonable doubt as to all charges, Eagleton looked directly at Holly, and said: "The accused's bogus story launched a massive search for the child and possible kidnapper that persisted over a long period of time. The accused's charade would not have been exposed if it had not been for her own father, who saw smoke coming from the accused's backyard, and while investigating the source, discovered the child's charred body. Upon being confronted by the discovery, the accused admitted to the fabrication as well as to having piled dry debris on top of her child and later setting the pile on fire. The forensic pathologist who performed the autopsy will testify that he found soot in the child's windpipe, meaning that the child was still alive at the time the child was set on fire."

Morrey observed Holly wilt in her chair and watched as Julia gently touched Holly's forearm obviously in a show of support.

Hesitating momentarily before returning to his seat, Eagleton added, "Justice cries out for guilty verdicts on all counts."

Julia, during the defense's opening statement, asked the jury to keep an open mind and not draw any conclusions until they had heard all the evidence. She then stated: "Even though an accused is not required to testify, Holly will do so in this case. She wants you to know the full story. The full story is that Holly found her daughter not breathing and without a pulse when she returned to the car. She tried to revive Missy but couldn't. She drove home thinking Missy might revive, but unfortunately she didn't. In a panic, she placed Missy in the garden in the backyard and piled dry twigs and grass clippings on top of her but was careful not to cover her face. Afraid to tell her husband, she drove back to the shopping center and reported her daughter missing. Later, when she was sure no one was watching, she returned to the backyard and again tried to revive Missy but to no avail. Hoping for a miracle, she repeated the process. For the next several days, she attempted to revive Missy even though it was futile. It became an obsession, and everything was as if she were in a trance watching the events unfold on a movie screen."

Julia continued by saying: "Since Holly couldn't accept the fact that Missy was dead, she didn't really consider her so-called cover-up as being deceptive. From the moment she found Missy unresponsive, and even at the time of her arrest, she felt like a robot, functioning without being functional. Even later, when she set fire to the debris covering Missy, she didn't consider it a finality. It was done not to destroy the evidence, but to make everything go away."

In conclusion, Julia stated: "Holly had always wanted a child of her own and adored her baby. She also adored her husband and didn't want to hurt him. She snapped when she found Missy unresponsive and she literally lost all connection with reality. Even now she has a compulsion to return to her backyard and try to revive her 'sleeping' baby. She did not wittingly cause her child's death and is guilty only of an error in judgment that was compounded by grief, a lack of acceptance of reality, and a desire to spare her husband and her daughter's grandparents the same grief.

"The loss of the baby she carried in her womb for nine months is punishment enough," Julia said. While fixing a determined gaze on the jury, she concluded by saying, "I hope you will agree and will return a verdict that is fair and just."

Morrey watched as Holly sat stone still. She appeared to be in another world. *Probably distancing herself from the nightmare*, Morrey speculated.

The prosecution was caught between a rock and a hard spot. The prosecution's forensic pathologist had issued a written report stating

Missy was alive when she was burned. And the only evidence of burning was a number of days later following the missing child report. Either she died on the date she was reported missing or she lay in a shallow grave for a number of days without nourishment and while weathering the elements then died. With the testimony of the defense's forensic pathologist, it was an easy call for the jury on the manslaughter charge.

• • •

On the manslaughter charge and the lesser included charge of criminally negligent homicide, Holly was found not guilty. Surprisingly, she was also found not guilty on the child abuse charge. On the other charges, the jury was deadlocked and unable to reach a verdict. Judge Bisben declared a mistrial on those charges. On the criminal homicide and child abuse charges, Holly was vindicated but faced a retrial on the other charges.

When the jury was interviewed by the attorneys afterward, they all stated without exception that they were persuaded to acquit on the criminal homicide charge on the basis of the testimony of the two pathologists who testified that there was no evidence of broken bones or that the baby had ever been abused except for the attempt to burn the body. They did not consider Holly to be a child abuser. Several of the jurors also added they were further persuaded to acquit by Holly's demeanor on the witness stand and her testimony that she would never take a breathing, cooing, and live baby and set fire to it, let alone her own flesh and blood.

The prosecution had enough and heard enough on the so-called baby burning case. When Morrey and Julia proposed a deferred judgment and sentence on the false reporting and concealment of death charges, the district attorney's office was more than willing. Holly, therefore, entered pleas of guilty to both charges in exchange for an agreement that the guilty pleas would be held in abeyance for a period of two years. If, at the end of the two-year period, she was determined to have abided by all the terms and conditions imposed pursuant to the deferred judgment and sentence, she could withdraw her pleas, and both charges would be dismissed. Otherwise, convictions would enter, and she would be sentenced accordingly. No one clamored for Eagleton's ouster, and everyone felt the disposition was warranted considering the unique circumstances of the case.

• • •

After Holly's case was concluded and she walked away a liberated woman, Morrey and Julia questioned if indeed she would ever be liberated or whether she would be haunted the rest of her life with the memory of the baby girl, who through no fault of the baby's own, was whisked away into eternity without having had the opportunity of experiencing God's wondrous provisions on earth. "Holly," Julia commented, "suffered double-fold: first when she indirectly caused the death of her baby and secondly when she was criminally prosecuted for having done so."

"Having to face the baby's daddy and grandparents, from my perspective, would be like facing a firing squad," Morrey commented. "I can't even imagine, on top of everything, how Holly was able to maintain her sanity."

"With a supportive husband like Ryan, despite his wife's almost unforgivable acts of grievous indiscretion, Holly was able to rebound."

"Ryan certainly was Holly's pillar of strength throughout the whole ordeal. Without his unconditional love, forgiveness, and understanding, I don't think she would have survived."

"The same thing was true of Missy's grandparents. Just think, it was Holly's father who exposed the charade," Julia said shaking her head. "Can you imagine what must have been going through his mind when he made that awful decision to call the authorities? Talk about balancing the equities and doing the right thing!"

"I'm not sure my character would be strong enough to turn in my daughters," Morrey admitted. "Lloyd Davies certainly deserves a lot of credit."

"Dad, I know exactly what you mean. I'm afraid if I were faced with the decision, I would do as you probably would do. I would opt to keep mum, rationalizing that I've already lost one granddaughter and by turning in my daughter, I would not only be losing one member of the family, but in essence, would be losing two. There's no way to trade one life for another; only trade two of his most beloved possessions, as Holly's father saw it, for honor."

"Well put, my precious daughter. It's a dilemma I hope none of us ever has to face."

"I guess we always have to do the right thing and hope for the best," Julia said somberly.

"We don't always do the right thing at the right moment, unfortunately. I guess wisdom is gleaned from our mistakes. Remember when you were ten years old, and I came home from the district attorney's office very dejected over having lost the case involving the father who experimented with natural medicines in lieu of insulin for his thirteen-year-old daughter, and she died?"

Julia nodded.

"Well, it's taken me Holly's case to realize I was wrong. Normally, a parent will do everything in his or her power to do what is best for his or her child. That's nature's way. However, despite what parents say, they're not infallible. They, too, sometimes make bad decisions! Even the law recognizes that in the business community a mere error in judgment does not in and of itself make the director or officer of a corporation, for example, liable. That, as you remember from your law classes, is the business judgment rule. If we can excuse the so-called experts who have all that training and experience from simple negligence, why not parents? Sometimes emotion gets in the way of better judgment."

"Is that an admission or a confession?" asked Julia. "It sounds as though you're saying the jury did the right thing in accepting the father's error in judgment defense and in acquitting him in the case you mentioned."

"Absolutely," said Morrey. "The jury had more compassion and understanding than I did. Having a *license to convict* doesn't give me the right to impose my beliefs on the criminal justice system. Thank God we have a check and balance system. Otherwise, the prosecutor would be the judge, jury and executioner, and we would be back to the feudal system where the king could do no wrong."

"I'm sure the district attorney's office thought they were doing the right thing when they prosecuted Holly. It took a jury to temper Eagleton's power, much like the jury in the alternative medical treatment case."

"Julia, it occurred to me in preparing Holly's defense that the predicament that Holly found herself in was one in which any of us could find ourselves. She made thousands of very valid decisions in her life. She was a gifted child, talented, intelligent, and wise. By making one error in judgment and then compounding it by a series of bad decisions, her whole life changed. She and those around her will never be the same. It's amazing how a small rock can make such exaggerated ripples. I pray that never happens to you or to your sister. Life can change in the blink of an eye. Look what ripples I have experienced as a result of a ricocheted bullet."

"Dad, that worried me as well. I knew a law student at CU who partied too much the last semester of his senior year, and having forced himself on a coed at a party, was charged with sexual assault. In his drunken stupor, he assaulted the arresting police officer and was charged with a felony. With only months left to graduate, he was expelled, and no other law school would admit him. Last I heard, he was working as a short-order cook in a restaurant in Park City. His whole life was turned upside down as a result of too much to drink. One night was all it took of the almost ten thousand nights in his life to destroy his whole future."

"Wasn't it Benjamin Franklin who said 'a little neglect may breed mischief '?" Morrey asked.

"I'm sure it was." Julia replied. "I know he postulated what we were taught was 'the importance of one.' But I don't remember anything more than that."

"Don't ask me why I remember this, but I do," Morrey quipped. "Ben, in trying to make his point, said, 'For want of a nail, the shoe was lost; for want of a shoe, the horse was lost; for want of a horse, the rider was lost; for want of a rider, the battle was lost; for want of the battle, the kingdom was lost—all for the want of a nail.'"

"Well, it's obvious that small things do make a difference and that an accumulation of a lot of small things makes a *big* difference," Julia interjected. "Isn't that exactly what happened in Holly's case? And isn't that what you preached to Theresa and me all our lives?"

"There are a lot of *ifs* in life," said Morrey. "*If* Missy hadn't been sick the night before, Holly wouldn't have left her in the car unattended; *if* Missy had been awake, Holly would have taken her into the store; *if* it hadn't been July, the temperature outside wouldn't have been in the nineties; *if* the temperature outside hadn't been scorching, it wouldn't have been scorching inside the car; *if* Holly had only cracked the windows, it wouldn't have been so stifling inside, and Missy would have had some relief; *if* Holly hadn't overextended her shopping, she would have returned to the car sooner and presumably in time to prevent what happened; *if* Holly hadn't panicked and had driven Missy to the ER, instead of home, Missy might have been revived; and *if* Holly hadn't hatched the elaborate scheme, she probably wouldn't have been prosecuted for any crime with the exception of maybe child neglect."

"That's a lot of ifs," said Julia pensively.

"As you said," continued Morrey, "'the accumulation of a lot of foibles makes for big trouble'."

"If Holly had been thinking straight, none of it would have happened," said Julia. "Being up late and not getting enough sleep, I know, handicaps me. I can't concentrate, and I don't think clearly the next day. And being up all night with a sick child has to make the symptoms even worse. Holly was clearly acting under disability—the same as someone who was doing drugs or had too much to drink. And what role her postpartum depression played is something we may never know."

"The culpable mental state, of course, is as much a part of the crime as the act itself," said Morrey. "Holly committed an act. Whether she had the requisite culpable mental state is something we question and something the jury obviously questioned as well. Clearly the prosecution didn't prove beyond a reasonable doubt that Holly had the requisite culpable mental state. If they had, the jury would have returned a guilty verdict on all charges."

"Holly's case goes to show that bad things can happen to good people," said Julia. "We're all used to reading about others accused of indiscretions. We never stop to think that maybe we will see our names or the names of someone near and dear to us in the blotter of the next issue of the daily news or maybe even in the headlines. We can be very judgmental and unsympathetic, unless of course, it involves us or someone close to us."

"What's the Bible say?" asked Morrey. "Isn't it 'Condemn not lest ye be condemned' or words to that effect?"

"Sounds like pretty good advice to me!" Julia said and shrugged. "But how many will heed the warning? And who was it who said, 'To err is human, to forgive divine'?"

Morrey smiled, "I don't remember. But whoever it was knew what he or she was talking about."

CHAPTER 18

Time to Say Good-bye

The funeral procession wound its way through the main streets of Las Cruces on its way to Sacred Heart Cemetery. Businesses had been closed that Friday in honor of Morrey's death. Only five years earlier, they had welcomed him back to his hallowed home; now they were paying their final respects.

The preceding Friday was Good Friday, and Morrey had been sitting in the San Juan Catolica Mision with the rest of the family, observing the memory of Christ's journey to Calvary and Christ's death on the cross. Its prophetic significance would not become apparent until the following day.

Saturday, while exiting the church after having gone to confession, Morrey's heart stopped beating, and he went to be with the Lord. He was carried back into the church and given the last rites.

Morrey was only sixty-two years of age and gave no hint that his time was up. Morrey had often said everyone was born with an expiration date, but no one knew for certain when it was. Morrey's cause of death was listed as pulmonary arrest or heart failure, and the family requested that no autopsy be performed. *Was there any better time to die than after you had just made peace with the Lord?* The next day, of course, was Easter Sunday, the Christian feast day commemorating the resurrection of Jesus the Christ. Was the timing coincidental or was God with Morrey the whole time, as Morrey had often claimed?

At Morrey's funeral, there was standing room only. Morrey's pallbearers consisted mainly of family members. Father Edmond Marques, now Monsignor Edmond Marques and in his late eighties, presided at the funeral mass and service.

Morrey's two daughters gave a joint eulogy. Theresa, now thirty-nine, favored her father in looks but favored her mother in equanimity and self-assuredness. Obviously struggling with her emotions, she began, "Dad had always been our pillar of strength and someone Julia and I had always admired and respected. He was stern but loving and understanding; encouraging but not demanding; and instructive but not dominating. He had always been there to celebrate our joy and there to comfort and console us in our sorrow. We couldn't have picked a more ideal father. The thing I remember most about him was that he was always optimistic and viewed the world in a bright light."

Theresa, dabbing at her eyes with a tissue, went on to state, "Dad could find something good in everyone and everything. Even after the capitol disaster, he never lost his positive attitude. Shortly after hearing the bad news, he told the family that now he wouldn't have to get his shoes resoled. He liked to laugh and tell jokes. He loved the outdoors and could hardly wait for the weekends to hunt, fish, camp, ski, skate, swim, work in the yard, and just be with family. Even confined to a wheelchair, he found a way to interact with his grandchildren and to go to Grandma and Grandpa Santana's cabin. His *family* not only included his daughters but the other loves of his life: his loving wife, mother, sister, in-laws, numerous relatives and friends—including all of you."

Theresa concluded by saying, "Although my father has gone to another paradise, his heart and his spirit will remain here always."

• • •

Julia, now thirty-seven, who looked more like her mother but was impulsive and inexorable like her father, also recounted some touching childhood memories.

"I attribute my legal career to Dad and my values to both of my parents. Dad was someone I always wanted to emulate. I tried to follow

Dad's advice and refer to what Theresa and I call *Daddyites*. One Daddyite was advice my grandfather had given Dad when he was just a boy: *You can be whatever you set your mind to be, but you have to be willing to pay the price.* Another was, *Once you lose your self-respect, you've lost everything.* There were others including a quote from Dad's favorite source, Benjamin Franklin: *Dust thou love life? Then do not squander time, for that's the stuff life is made of."*

Julia was having difficulties stifling her emotions and had to take a moment to dry her tears. Since she was a lawyer and knew what was expected of a lawyer, she expounded on the virtues that she observed in her father in his role as both a prosecutor and as a defense attorney.

"My father always emphasized that one's word was his or her bond and that promises were meant to be kept. He also gave the following advice: *Don't compromise your ideals; Don't risk a lot for a little; Choose your battles; Only fight for what is important; You'll only get as good as you give; If you don't prepare for everything, you prepare for failure; Take a shortcut, and it will take you twice as long to get there; Don't jump without a parachute or safety line; Never box yourself into the corner; Never underestimate your opponent;*

Never trust the outcome to luck; Keep trying until you succeed; and Never give up!"

She concluded by saying her father was particularly emphatic about the role of a power broker. His advice was simple: *Never abuse your power! Don't warlord over those whom you have power!*

Sergio, the rock upon which the family relied, had a difficult time in what was listed as the "Personal Segment." Now in his eighties and having hung up his sheriff 's badge many years before, he appeared frail and tentative. Morrey had been like his son, and he couldn't have loved him more. It was obvious he felt compelled to say something.

Sergio began: "I cannot begin to express my true feelings for the man who married my beloved daughter. He was more than a son-in-law; he was more like a son. Working with him in law enforcement all those years made me appreciate his worth. If he told you something, you could bank on it. If he told you he would do something, you could depend on it. And if he made a decision, you could bet your life on it. The quality I admired most in Morrey's professional life was his conscious effort in not abusing his prosecutorial discretion. Even though he had a *license to convict* and may have even had a motive to abuse his discretion from time to time, he kept sacred the trust implicit in his office. His role was to seek justice, and justice is what he attained. Never did he vary from that course nor violate his oath of office. He entered this earth a favored son, and he departed this earth as a favored son, husband, father, and friend."

Monsignor Marques, as a concluding prayer, asked the Almighty to temper justice with mercy in heaven "just as our dearly beloved tempered justice with mercy on this earth." He then quoted from the Bible: *Blessed is he who maintains justice and constantly does what is right.*

Margarita, accompanied by Monique, removed the ankh from her neck, and retrieving a rosary given to her by Morrey's father, lovingly placed both items in Morrey's crossed hands. She, along with Monique, kissed Morrey a tender transitory good-bye. She then prayed in a low voice, "Father God. You gave your only begotten son for me. Now, I give you my only son. You have favored him in life, and now I pray that you favor him in death and for all time."

Morrey's casket was then closed, and he would go to the grave, clutching the symbols of his love for his God and his family and his devotion to the Blessed Virgin Mary.

The mourners had said their own transitory

good-byes and silent prayers. In doing so, they knew beyond doubt that Morrey had fought the good fight, finished the race, and kept the faith and was now wearing the crown of righteousness that he so justly deserved.

• • •

At the gravesite, the mourners witnessed a sight that would become part of their folklore. Perched on one end of Morrey's casket was an eagle and on the other end a dove. No one saw either land or fly away. They, too, had symbolism in Morrey's life. The eagle stood for honor, bravery, and justice. The dove stood for peace and love.

When Morrey departed his earthly Paraiso and entered the gates of his heavenly Paraiso, he had an approval rating of a lofty 100%! Things couldn't get any better than that—especially for a former prosecutor. In the last analysis, it would not all have been in vain!